THE WITCH'S INHERITANCE

A SILVER MIST COVE COZY MYSTERY
BOOK ONE

LYSSA LUND

WHIMSEY PUBLISHING

For my daughters, my sisters and my nieces—may you always know the magic in your spirit, the strength in your hearts, and the power of your stories.

PROLOGUE

T *wenty-Five Years Ago*

WE WERE BEING HUNTED.

Clutching the book to my chest, I looked wildly around. There was no moon tonight. At the beginning of our evening, the darkness had seemed mysterious and perfect. Now, it was inspiring panic and terror. We'd already gone deeper into the forest than I'd ever been before, and I had no idea which direction would take us back to town.

Or that we would make it back before we were caught.

"Let's go back," my companion whispered, her voice carrying through the forest. I winced. "My dad will find us before morning. We just need to hide."

If we went back, we might lure whoever was hunting us. I didn't know why, but letting anyone else find the cave was a terrible idea — how was I going to tell them that?

We couldn't go back and hide because of a *feeling* that I had. I was the reason that we were out here, to begin with.

Stupid, stupid, stupid.

Helena would kill me when she found out. Of course, that was assuming I was still alive.

We couldn't keep stumbling through the forest, blind. Reluctantly, I turned back and followed my friend's lead until the cave was in sight. It felt like such an oddly sacred place. Maybe it would keep us safe.

"Got 'em," someone shouted. Someone else screamed. Ginger? On impulse, I opened my mouth to follow suit, and a hand clamped around my upper arm. The book was yanked out of my hands, and a sharp pain exploded in my head.

Darkness.

And then...well, then, the monsters came.

Red-eyed demons, cackling and shrieking at the top of their lungs. The sound echoed off the cave walls, punctuated only by the gushing water.

The cave. We were back in the cave, and we weren't alone.

Paris, help us! Help us!

Ginger. Sage. I had to get them. Had to help them, but where were they? Everywhere I looked, something hissed at me from the darkness.

Then fog. So much heavy fog.

"She's fighting it. Hit her with it again."

"How is she fighting it? She's just a teenager!"

"Just knock her out."

Darkness.

And then the monsters came back.

CHAPTER 1
PARIS

It's time to come home.

That voice. One she hadn't heard in years. Obviously, she was dreaming.

"I *am* home," she told Helena, a note of annoyance in her voice.

Please. You've only been here a year, and you're already bored.

"I'm a little old for you to be judging me, don't you think?" Paris muttered even as she accepted the absurdity of the situation. She was talking to the disembodied voice of a woman she hadn't seen in twenty years.

Tell me what you see.

A dream. It had to be a dream, and yet Paris still looked out the window and sighed. She knew the place that the dream was trying to show her. Silver Mist Cove. She'd only ever seen it in the summers, but something about the small town had left a mark.

Of course, since she was dreaming, her mind was also just recreating what she thought Silver Mist Cove looked like. Even if things had changed since she had last been in town, there was no way that the bed and breakfast Rose ran was actually that lurid shade of pink.

Tell me what you see.

"Still so demanding," Paris muttered. "I'm looking at the town. At the inn. At..."

Her voice trailed off as a figure emerged from the inn. Two figures. Shrouded in darkness, but there was something in the swagger of the taller one that made her heart skip a beat, even after all this time.

He needs you.

"He is probably married with 2.5 kids, four dogs, and a trophy from last year's annual neighborhood barbecue contest."

They all need you. It's time to come home, Paris. Time to find the truth.

Suddenly, clouds descended from the sky and covered the town. It thickened, darkened. The two figures standing in front of the bed and breakfast were the last things she saw before the darkness overtook them as well.

"I am so sorry about that! We're still arguing about the faucet designs, of all things."

At the sound of her client's voice, Paris blinked, and the image in front of her faded completely. In the here and now, she stood in front of the large picture window that overlooked a courtyard painted in the orange hues of the fading sunset. She could see why Lance was thinking of putting a gazebo out there. It had some powerful romantic vibes.

"Paris, are you all right?"

Clearing her throat, Paris turned. She'd experienced some strange things in the buildings she helped decorate, but a waking vision was a new one for her. It wouldn't have anything to do with this newly renovated manor-turned bed and breakfast. From the moment she'd stepped in the doors, she'd felt nothing but cheer and joy. The building was happy at the prospect of being alive again, of having a purpose.

No, the vision had come from her own imagination. She really was going to have to talk to her doctor about changing her anxiety medication. Working on one bed and breakfast was making her think of another from a lifetime ago. A lifetime better left to the memories of others.

"Just soaking in the view," she chirped. "And I can assure you that arguing over faucet designs is perfectly normal. It's caring about the details that make something like this work. You'd be surprised how many bed and breakfast reviews talk about the bath and showers."

Lance grinned. He and his wife had been planning on opening a bed and breakfast since before they were married. Now, for their seventh wedding anniversary, they were making it a reality.

"Anyway, here is your check. We really can't thank you enough for all the help you've given us. We would never have seen our dream become a reality if it weren't for you. You really have a knack for this kind of thing."

Paris accepted the check and neatly tucked it away in her folder. "This was a pleasure project for me. I've spent the year helping to design office after office. It's nice to work on something warmer for a change. Now, please don't hesitate to let me know if you have any questions from here on out. You can even email me with pictures if you two start butting heads again."

"Thank you so much, and you can be sure we'll be dropping your name and business card whenever anyone compliments the decor."

With one last glance over her shoulder, just to make sure that the courtyard was still there and not some faded memory of Silver Mist Cove, Paris said goodbye and headed out to her car.

As much as she enjoyed working with Lance and Ashley, she was glad the job was done. Her own hesitation and second-guessing made her realize that it was time to take a break before the burn-out hit. She'd been taking projects back-to-back for the last two years since her mother's death.

She felt a little itch to take a step back and reevaluate. Especially since that project at the beginning of the year, a tech company's office renovation. Something about the building made the hairs on the back of her neck stand up, and she still hadn't recovered.

The drive back to her apartment took less than twenty minutes. Part of her knew the irony of renting instead of buying. The generic apartments were always so bland, and they challenged her creativity. She had enough money to consider a mortgage, and it was stupid to continue to throw money at renting, but honestly, she just had trouble settling down.

Was this the town where she would finally put down roots? Doubtful. Her lease was up in three months, and she was already considering the next place.

Sharp barks pierced the quiet morning as she made her way up the sidewalk. It was Sugar, greeting her after her quick morning outing.

Okay, if she were being honest, Sugar had probably been barking the whole time, but the pudgy white chihuahua was always happy to see her no matter how long she'd been away.

Humming to herself, she took out her keys and opened the door. From his pink fluffy bed on the leather couch,

Sugar barked again and wiggled his body. "Let me change, and we'll go for a walk!"

Kicking off her pumps, Paris exchanged the skirt and blouse for a pair of sweatpants and a tee shirt. Sliding into her sneakers, she picked up the leash and turned. Sugar hadn't gotten off his bed. Instead, he'd just rolled over and exposed his belly.

"No," Paris said firmly. "The vet says you need to lose weight, so we are going on a walk. Come."

He wiggled.

"Sugar, come here. Now."

He growled.

"You want a cookie?"

With a happy yip, the chihuahua rolled over and tore down the ramp toward her. Shaking her head, Paris grabbed a cookie and used it to lure the pooch into a harness.

Sidewalks wound all around the apartment complex, but there was very little that was interesting on the grounds. A water feature had been added at the back of the complex, but it wasn't well maintained, so it was just a littered mosquito pit. Paris preferred the walk that led to the shopping center across the street, but the heat made the asphalt dangerous for little paws.

So they meandered. Her heart wasn't into the walk anyway. It took a few minutes to realize that she was humming and another minute to realize *what* she was humming.

That Hanson song that had been so popular when she was sixteen. She, Sage, and Ginger had played it a million times that summer, even choreographing a dance to it. The memory brought a smile to her face, followed by a wave of sadness.

The fury was gone. It used to just sit in the middle of her chest and pulse at odd times, but it had been twenty years. Twenty years since her summers in Silver Mist Cove when her parents dropped her off with their good friend Helena and jetted off overseas.

Twenty years since her bonded friendship was shattered.

Since the *event* happened and, the whole town turned against her.

So the anger was gone, but the lingering questions not only remained but grew stronger over these past few years. Helena was a family friend. Enough of a family friend that from the age of eight until she was eighteen, Paris spent summers with her. Yet, when she'd asked her parents about how they met, her mom had just waved her hand and said *oh, she was a friend of my mother's.*

That was it. That was all the explanation Paris had gotten. She hadn't found it suspicious then. She was only eleven or maybe twelve when she'd asked the question, and the reason had been good enough for her.

Then, the event happened, and Helena couldn't wait fast enough to get Paris out of town. Her parents had never said a word about it. She went to college and tried to forget it happened. What she had needed was therapy, someone to talk to, but that never happened.

Helena never reached out.

Her father died about five years later. A car accident that took him unexpectedly. Helena didn't show up at the funeral.

Someone from Silver Mist Cove had reached out. Helena's good friends Duke and Annie Banns. They'd started writing letters to Paris that summer, letting her know how much they missed her. How they wished she'd come back and visit.

She wrote, but she never went back, and they never talked about Helena.

But then her mother died. A cancer diagnosis that she fought for only three months before it took her. Paris would never forget the words she spoke to her that night.

"I should have told you. We thought Helena could help, but then...oh, it all went so wrong. I have so many regrets, Paris, but I love you. I hope you know that."

Of course, Paris knew that her mother loved her. Why would she think anything differently? She could be cold sometimes and didn't like to discuss the hard and emotional things, but that was normal for lots of mothers and daughters. Her mother had insinuated that there was a *problem*. A reason, other than needing a long-term babysitter, that her parents had to send her to Helena.

Thinking for sure that Helena would show up to her mother's funeral, Paris prepared herself to ask the hard questions.

But once again, Helena didn't show. Didn't call. Didn't write.

Heavy black smoke rose from the ground. It came on suddenly, or maybe she was just so lost in her own thoughts that she didn't realize it was happening until it was billowing around her waist.

"Sugar. Sugar!" Paris cried out. Reaching down, she snagged the chihuahua, who gave her an annoyed look.

Stumbling back, Paris looked wildly around. A car door slammed in the parking lot. The owner slowly pocketed his keys and made his way to his apartment as if he wasn't sliding through a blanket of darkness.

Voices to her left. She looked over and saw someone on

their front porch, talking on the phone. No panic in their voice.

Was she losing her mind? Tightening her grip on Sugar, she moved slowly toward her apartment and focused on her breathing. No anxiety attacks. Just deep breaths. In. Out. In. Out

Her pocket buzzed. Paris blinked, and the smoke was gone. Completely. Not even a single tendril rising from the sidewalk.

Sugar struggled, flinging his chubby body back and forth to try to wiggle out of Paris's hold, so Paris put him down. Her pocket continued to buzz.

Slowly. Paris pulled her phone out and stared at the caller ID.

Annie.

Swallowing hard, she answered. "Hello?"

"Paris? Oh, Paris. I wasn't even sure if this number would work for you. Duke's office is a mess, like usual, and you know how we are with phones."

"I'm here."

"Paris, honey, I'm so sorry. There's been...well...something has happened. Sweetheart, Helena is dead."

CHAPTER 2
FINN

Amidst the colorful specialty shops and mystical cafes, there were mundane services in Silver Mist Cove. They weren't nearly as flashy, and they struggled since they didn't draw tourists. Some of them tried to have a foot in both worlds. If Finn's memory served correctly, the paint shop had a reasonably successful service where an aura reader assisted customers who wanted to match their paint job with their mystical energy.

The Law Offices of Turner and Addams didn't even attempt to feed into the hype. In fact, the two partners were well known around town because when they first got together to open the office, they advertised legal consultation for suing psychics who gave terrible advice. That was a long time ago, and they'd since learned to live more in harmony with their neighbors.

As Danny Turner read the contents of Helena's will to Finn, her only surviving family, the lawyer still looked a bit out of place. Danny was cut and dry in his grey suit and blue tie, and he was probably wearing the only set of gold cufflinks and Cole Hahn loafers in Silver Mist Cove. Yet the words that had come out of his mouth were one hundred percent, Helena, as if she were dressing Finn down just like she had when he was a child. It was an oddly dissonant experience.

In the end, Finn stared at Danny. "So that's it, then?"

"You can contest it, of course. It will take time, years even, but yes. That's it. Legally, this stands."

Finn walked out of the boring grey and white office hidden in the bright yellow strip with those words ringing in his head.

Legally, this stands.

Helena never cared about what was legal. She'd probably laugh at that. What she would tell him was that he wasn't to question her and just to go along with what she said.

As a teenager, he'd pushed back on that sentiment hard. In his twenties and thirties, he'd just smiled indulgently and let her do what she wanted so long as it didn't seem to stir up too much trouble.

But now...oh, now he had questions. Too bad she wasn't around now to give him any answers. No doubt Helena had planned that perfectly.

The drive from downtown to the coast was a short one. About half an hour, but then, Silver Mist Cove wasn't exactly a sprawling town. Most of the tourists were forced to stay in the surrounding villages and drive in. Traffic had become such a nightmare that now there were buses that went to nearby hotels to pick people up and drop them off. Bids for undeveloped lands were astronomically high as land developers tried to take advantage, but most of the land belonged to some of the oldest families in Silver Mist and wasn't likely to ever be sold.

High on the bluffs, houses dotted the otherwise barren landscape. These houses were the subject of the famous Silver Mist Cove photographs, and amateurs came from miles to try to replicate them. During the time of the original photos, there was a spectacular lightning storm. In the black and white pictures taken several decades ago, a massive wave had splashed up in the background just as a streak of lightning came down. Rumors began that the mystical forces of Silver Mist came from those storms. Energy swirling vortexes that psychics were able to tap into.

Bullshit, all of it, but it made for great PR. In the summer, the town saw waves of tourists that didn't even dwindle in the fall. Shops closed their doors in the winter and early spring to get ready for the next tourist season. The locals took that time to breathe and huddle in their sanctuaries while psychics across the world submitted applications to the town council to perform on the main stage the following year.

What would those fake psychics and all those tourists think if they knew the truth?

Smiling to himself, Finn drove past the houses and turned right into a small neighborhood dotted with old-style Victorian manors. At the end of the cul-de-sac, Helena's yellow and brown house stood and almost reached out to him in greeting.

There was another car in the driveway.

Annoyed, Finn navigated his silver Porsche around it and stepped out. The license plate, which read *Sell 4 U,* told him exactly who was hustling around the house, no doubt peering in the windows.

"Mr. Ferryworth?" A man said brightly as he jumped down from the steps of the front porch.

"It's Whitlock, actually," Finn said neutrally. "And no, I'm not selling."

The agent ignored him as he pulled out his card. "Barry Weathers of Weather Realty. I don't think we've met yet."

"No, we have not, and again, I'm not selling."

"Sure, sure. I understand. It takes time to process death, especially the death of an institution like Helena Ferryworth. I am going to miss her cupcakes. I made sure to order a dozen at the beginning of every month. I still can't believe she's gone."

Finn just grunted. The man talked like Helena was a moss-covered statue or a museum.

"I am sure a man such as yourself has no plans to stay in town. I promise that we care about more than the dollar signs. These houses are like historic landmarks. They should stay local and go to someone who cares. That is the kind of thing that we care about, and we will do our very best to ensure that the buyer is worthy of such a home."

"Mr. Weathers..."

"Barry."

"Barry, I just got into town. I am short on patience, and I don't want to have to repeat myself a third time, so please leave my property. Now."

He still hadn't taken the business card that was in Barry's hands, but the agent was undeterred. "I understand. You have a nice evening, Mr. Whitlock. I'm just going to leave this right here for you. Beautiful car that you've got there. Just beautiful. Don't see many of those in a place like this," he chuckled, trying to drive home once more that Finn didn't belong here. After placing the card on the railing, he tipped his head and jaunted down the porch past Finn.

He took his time, no doubt hoping that Finn would

unlock the door and let him in, but Finn waited until the agent's car was gone before he fished his keys out of his pocket.

The lawyers gave him Helena's copies, but they were still in the envelope in the car. Finn had a copy, and unless something spectacular had happened in the last year to make Helena change the locks, it should fit.

It did. Taking a deep breath, Finn turned the key and opened the heavy wooden door as he stepped inside.

A breeze blew past him, carrying the air of impatience. Finn almost smiled as he glanced around the foyer. The slate floor was covered with an old maroon Persian runner with a cream fringe that Helena used to always fuss over when it was mussed. An antique dresser was on the side under a large brass-framed mirror. The familiar scent of rosemary reached out to him, and he almost stepped in front of the mirror and turned to look at it.

Almost. Once, when he was twelve and had tracked mud in the house, he looked in the mirror and lost ten years of his life when a mud monster stared back at him. Another time, as a teenager, he'd broken curfew and come in late, and when he looked in the mirror, there had been no reflection at all.

Ah, such interesting times here.

It occurred to him that never again would he hear his aunt fussing at him to close the door or stop messing with the talisman. He'd never listen to her demanding to know if he'd been making out with so-and-so's daughter at the pier again.

The woman *was* like an institution in his life. Even as she aged, she was still mentally as sharp as ever. Still physically strong. He couldn't believe she'd had a heart attack.

Sadness swept over him, and the air shifted around him

and seemed to embrace him. "Sorry. I can't. Not right now."

The energy released him mournfully as he stepped back and closed the door. After locking it, he walked around the back, unlocked the gate, and checked the backyard. Helena's gardens were looking greener than ever. Fresh baby greens cropped up from their dark soil, still wet from last night's rains and happy in the late spring air. If they felt the effects of their owner's passing, they showed no signs of it.

The back door was locked, and everything was in order. If he wasn't going to go inside, there was no point in hanging out for too long. By now, half the town probably knew that he was back, and soon, neighbors would be glancing out the window and seeing his car in the drive. They'd ask a bunch of questions and try to hug him.

He wasn't ready for that.

In fact, if it was up to him, he would have quietly sold the house, had the contents shipped to him, and only stepped foot in Silver Cove for the funeral. Easier that way.

But Helena hadn't wanted easy, apparently. She'd created a little chaos in her last move, and Finn was left to clean up the mess.

CHAPTER 3
PARIS

"Does he bark?"

Paris frowned as the young blonde woman typed with one hand on the computer. The other hand held up her head as if accepting guests at Silver Mist Cove's only bed-and-breakfast was the most boring job in the world.

Luckily, it wasn't tourist season. In about a month, the woman's blank expression wasn't going to cut it with the customers.

"Does that matter?"

"We pride ourselves on our quiet and peaceful atmosphere," the woman continued in a listless voice. "We cannot accept a barking dog."

But they could have screaming kids in the summer? Paris took a breath and tried to maintain a pleasant smile. She was probably the only guest in the bed-and-breakfast. "He doesn't make a peep."

Sugar growled in response, and the woman finally raised her head to get a good look at Paris. There was a jolt of recognition in Paris. "Are you Rose's granddaughter?"

"Yeah." The woman held out her hand. "Credit card?"

Paris wracked her brain. Rose, the owner, had a son who was a few years older than Paris. What was his name? "Gordon's daughter, right? It's been a long time since I've been here. How is he?"

"Fine."

"And your name is?" Paris prompted.

"Addy. Here you go, the room is on the second floor on the right. Wi-Fi password is TheWorld1234, capital T, capital W. Breakfast is between eight and ten."

Wasn't Addy a delight? Paris accepted the key, and when she turned around, a familiar figure was coming down the stairs. At the sight of her, Rose gasped.

"Paris? Paris Hollyman? That can't possibly be you."

"Hello, Rose," Paris said with a forced smile. The truth was that she'd been pleased that Rose wasn't at the desk when she checked in. The bed and breakfast owner was known for her gossipy nature. Now that Rose knew that Paris was here, half the town would be informed within the hour.

"Oh, my dear, you must be here because of Helena. Her death has really cast a shadow over this town."

Black smoke choking out the town.

Paris mentally shoved the image out of her head. "Yes, I imagine it has. If you don't mind, I'm going to get settled. I've been driving for eight hours, and I need a shower and to head out and grab some food."

"Oh, of course, of course. There will be plenty of time to catch up," Rose said as she pulled her phone out of her bright purple dress pocket. "May your stay be as pleasant as the blooms of a rose."

"Clever," Paris managed as she carried her luggage and a quietly snarling Sugar by Rose and up the steps. There were only two doors on the second landing, so it was easy enough to find her room.

Like most of the businesses in Silver Mist, the rooms were catered to the theme. There were large tarot card prints framed on the wall. This room was the sun and the world. The room colors were just as bright and cheery with yellows and greens. The four-poster bed was a little out of date, but it was all very charming.

Paris wasn't there for charm. She was there for answers. Since she couldn't get them from Helena, she had a plan B. Sneak into Helena's house and search for the journals that Helena meticulously kept. Hopefully, she could get in tonight and get them out before Finn arrived. She'd already driven by the house and was pleased to see that the driveway was empty.

Shower first. Then food and a walk around town. Since she didn't exactly have permission to be in Helena's house, she'd need to go under the cover of night.

As MUCH AS her blood pumped for action, the drive had taken a lot out of her, and it was two hours before she, with her leashed Sugar, made it out of the bed and breakfast. The desk was suspiciously deserted, but Paris took a moment to check out the pamphlets. As much as the world outside had changed, Silver Mist Cove, apparently, had not.

Center Yourself- and pick up the essentials at Gia's Grocery

Maeve's Mystical Tours: All the secrets Silver Mist has to offer (and discover the true magic of the town)

Call Master Rick for the best hairstyle to fit your face and your horoscope!

Helena's Cupcakes mouthful of magic.

Paris paused at that last one. Helena had started to

advertise to tourists? That was new. She used to hide away during tourist seasons. Paris did all the heavy lifting when it came to running errands and delivering the baked goods during the summer. She would constantly question why Helena lived in such a tourist trap if she hated tourists.

Helena would only wave away the question and mutter something under her breath.

Sugar was starting to circle, so Paris tugged the leash and managed to get the dog through the hotel doors just before he relieved himself on the shag rug.

Outside, the sun was starting to set. Here, there was still a hint of chill in the air, and Paris could at least be grateful for leaving the southern heat behind. Even in the summer, Silver Mist always had a lovely breeze coming in off the Pacific Ocean. The weather patterns were so perfect it was almost bizarre. Rain was almost invariably a refreshing mist. The only heavy downpours seemed to happen offshore, where the waves seemed to whip up violent storms, but those storms rarely made it to land.

Rose's Bed and Breakfast was front and center of Main Street. Without even thinking, Paris turned left. Sage's father used to run Jack's Brews, the only bar in town, and he always made the best sandwiches. After morning deliveries, Paris would meet Sage and Ginger at the bar for lunch, and then they'd sit in on the early afternoon shows at the theater. Ginger's mother was one of the performers, but she was a big headliner, so she usually performed at night. Despite that, the girls always poked fun at the performances.

Paris hadn't even realized how much she missed that until she realized where she was walking. Stopping short, she turned abruptly to head down one of the side streets. Some of the food trucks would still be in operation, and she was better off grabbing something to-go than to head into a bar or restaurant. She was too antsy to sit anyway.

At Taco and Tarot, Paris stopped and grinned. A head popped out the window. "Paris Hollyman, that is you!"

At first, Paris thought maybe she was dreaming. That was Bobby Woods in the food truck. But there was no way Bobby Woods would have a food truck. She was sure he probably didn't even have a legal license. Apparently, at some point in the eighties, he'd come to Silver Mist with his wife, had some sort of spiritual awakening, and refused to leave. He named himself the unofficial town welcomer and often showed tourists around, encouraging them to "give up your earthly possessions like me and absorb the mystical energies of the town!"

All of this came at a price, of course. He did indeed live without much. The last Paris had seen of him; he'd been living at the edge of the woods near the middle school.

He was the first person they saw when she, Sage, and Ginger emerged from the forest three nights after going missing with no memory of what had happened to them.

"Bobby," Paris managed. "You have a food truck."

Stating the obvious. *Way to go, Paris.* But, honestly, she didn't know what to say.

"I do! About ten years now! Tacos and Tarot. Clever, right?"

"Sure. Yes. Very clever. So I get a reading with my taco?"

"You sure do! What would you like?"

After a quick glance at the menu — she really didn't want to linger for too long for obvious reasons — she ordered a burrito. Bobby yelled her order towards the back of the truck and then grabbed a deck of cards.

He was going to do a reading for her right here? She

resisted the urge to look over her shoulder. Usually, readings were private. What did he do if there was a line?

"Hey, Sooz! Look who it is," Bobby called out, and Paris stopped resisting and turned her head.

Oh. Oh, no. There were several people coming up behind her. No, more than several.

This was no coincidence. Every single one of them had their phone in their hands, and their gazes were laser-locked onto her.

She recognized faces even if she couldn't remember names. Locals.

"All right," Bobby said as he shuffled cards. "Let's see what's in store for you. You're here for Helena's funeral, right?"

"Bobby, you really don't have to do the reading."

"Of course I do. It comes with the service. Says so right on the truck. Don't want to cheat Silver Mist Cove's most famous resident."

"Not a resident," she managed. "And really, I'm in a hurry, so..."

"Ah, first card. The Hard-Shell. Your past has seen some cracks in it, but then, I guess that's common knowledge."

The Hard-Shell? Were his tarot cards...taco themed?

"You've had a hard time moving past it, haven't you? Got little bits of it stuck in your teeth?"

Paris's cheeks heated as she felt the crowd gather behind her. "Bobby, I've been gone for twenty years. I think I've moved on."

"Maybe. Maybe. I'm just telling you what the cards say. Now then, as for your present...oh, the Under-Filled Taco. You won't find any of that in this food truck. Just saying. Helena's death has you down. We're feeling that too. So sad. So sad. But hey, it's brought you back, hasn't it?"

"Not that she should have come back," a voice said quietly behind her. "Wasn't like Helena wanted her, was it?"

Don't turn around. Don't turn around.

Sugar growled, and Paris took a deep breath. "And what do your taco cards say about my future, Bobby?"

After turning the last card, his eyes widened for dramatic effect. Knowing the showmanship of this town, Paris wasn't fooled. "Beans."

"Beans?"

"Oh, Paris, your future is as mysterious as beans. You never really quite know what kind of beans you're getting, do you? And how those beans are going to treat you. Could be painful. If you stay Paris, you could be in trouble. Real trouble. The beans card is nothing to mess around with."

Wonderful. Paris forced a smile. "I'll take my chances, Bobby. Thank you."

"Suit yourself. Here's your burrito, and for what it's worth, it's good to see you, Paris."

Accepting her food, Paris turned and found her way blocked. Hard eyes settled on her. "You thinking of stirring up trouble again?"

"I didn't stir up trouble then," she told the man patiently. He was trying to intimidate her, and she couldn't even remember his name. "Now then, if you'll excuse me, I have someplace to be."

The man suddenly jumped. "Oh! That little termite just bit me!"

"Sugar? You must be mistaken. He doesn't bite."

If she wasn't so hungry, she wouldn't have even eaten the burrito that had come with the dreaded beans card. Despite the absurdity of it, she did laugh to herself as she made her way back to the bed and breakfast.

Instead of going back to her room, she walked to her car. Night was falling, and it was the perfect time to head to Helena's.

Maybe she should have paid more attention to the tarot reading. Meditated on it. Asked Bobby for another reading. But she hadn't.

Instead, she pulled up to Helena's, carrying Sugar in her arms while she walked to the door, pulled out her key, and slid it in, wondering if it would still work.

It did.

And when she walked in, the shock hit her before she even understood what she was looking at.

Flashes of green seared her memory. Unsettled her. Sent her into a tailspin. She lost all sense of reality until someone's hands settled at her waist.

"Hello, Paris," a warmly familiar voice said behind her. "It's a little soon for you to be killing people, isn't it?"

"I..." she didn't dare turn around. She was more prepared to deal with the dead body sprawled out in front of her than the man at her back. "I found him like this."

"Of course you did," Finn sighed. "Well, Helena's house was always interesting. I suppose it shouldn't surprise me that there's a dead body in it."

CHAPTER 4
FINN

Finn knew that it was a mistake to put his hands on her, but something about the way she was standing in the open doorway and weaving back and forth told him that she was not okay.

Seeing the dead body in front of her made him a little not okay as well, but Paris was his priority. "Did you touch anything?" he asked her.

"What? Touch anything? I didn't kill him!" She was slowly snapping out of her panic, but her eyes kept darting to the body, and her complexion was paling quickly.

"I didn't say you did. Come back to the front porch." Gently, he pulled her back out of the house. Angry blue eyes stared at him, but the little white bundle in her arms didn't snap at him.

"Finn. You're here."

"I am." Good, she was finally taking in her surroundings. He guided her backward until she was on the porch swing. "Sit."

Obediently, she sat. That was his first clue that she was

25

not okay. Paris had never done anything he'd asked her to do in her life.

"Are you staying here?"

"Ah. Wondering now if I left that body?"

"What? No. I... there's a dead man in Helena's house!"

"There is. Stay here. I'm going to call the police."

"He's...he has monsters."

There was an odd tone in her voice, and Finn paused and looked over. Her gaze had shifted and softened, and she didn't even seem to be talking to him anymore. "Paris." He kept his voice as calm as possible. "Paris, are you still with me?"

"It's like an echo. Over and over again. Monsters."

The dog barked sharply, and Paris blinked and nodded. "The police. That's a good idea."

Never taking his eyes off her, Finn reported the body and slipped the phone back into his pocket despite the request that he stay on the line. Paris stroked her dog and refused to meet his eyes. "I didn't mean any disrespect," she said. "I didn't know you were here."

"You spent just as much time here as I did," Finn told her. "I don't consider it disrespectful that you wanted to see the house."

"Not recently." Sighing, she looked up at him. "So, how's life? Married with 2.5 kids and a man cave full of neighborhood barbecue medals?"

"Excuse me?"

"Sorry. Just trying to take my mind off things. How are you, Finn? It's been a long time."

It had been a long time. The pretty teenager had grown up into a pretty woman. More than pretty. Clearing his throat, Finn looked away. Now was not the time to note just how well Paris had grown up.

"Divorced. No kids. No man cave and no barbecue medals. Also, something about a man cave full of barbecue medals makes me think serial killer."

"True. I suppose it does have a strange sort of manic quality to it." She fell silent and stared at the door. "I can't believe she's gone. She was so full of life. So...big. Had she changed? No. Don't answer that. It's not appropriate. My mind is just wandering."

Finn fought the urge to sit next to her and put an arm around her. He'd wondered if Paris would show up. Helena talked about her so much, and Finn had told her to reach out, but she never did. She just muttered that it wasn't safe.

Not that Finn knew what she meant. Had Helena known what had happened to Paris and her friends?

It was the one summer he hadn't come. The summer after his and Helena's big fight. The summer that Paris went missing. When three teenage girls go missing for days, the nation takes notice, especially in a town as popular as Silver Mist Cove.

And when the nation takes notice, the FBI does as well. It wasn't just bad press that was bad for business. It also had the locals and the performers on edge. The psychic business was about showmanship.

And it was also about cons. There were some shady people in Silver Mist Cove. Then and now. They didn't appreciate being investigated.

So they turned their rage onto the three girls who claimed to have no memory of what happened. The town pointed their fingers and accused them of seeking attention.

Finn hadn't been there. It was his one regret.

"What about you? Married with 2.5 kids? And if you say

yes, I'm going to ask about what happened to that half of a kid."

"No. Never married. No kids. Not really the mothering type. Well, except for this guy. This is Sugar. He's my angel." Her voice trailed off as sirens sounded in the distance. "Did you get a good look at him?"

"Sugar. Sure. He's..." he was fat, partly bald, and looking at him with all the fury his little body could muster. "Cute. Real cute."

"No." The sirens were close. If Finn turned around, he could probably see their lights flashing as they drove down the bluffs. The locals were going to have plenty to say about the police making all that ruckus. The dead body wasn't any cause for an emergency. Discretion. That was what Silver Mist was all about. "The dead body."

Not only could Finn identify the dead body, but he'd noticed a few interesting things about the scene. "Saw enough."

"Beans," Paris sighed. "Stupid beans."

She was slipping back into shock, but when he stepped toward her, she stood and adjusted the dog in her arms. "Do you know who the sheriff is now?"

"Dobbs."

"Dobbs? As in Trevor Dobbs?"

"That's the one."

Her face fell. "This is going to be a long night."

Finn never got a chance to ask Paris what her history was with Dobbs, but it was clear from the sneer on his face when he walked up the steps that it wasn't a good history.

"First night in town and already calling the police, Paris?" The sheriff demanded. "It's a little early for that, don't you think?"

One step put Finn between Dobbs and Paris. "Actually, I was the one who called you. On account of the dead body in my aunt's foyer."

Dobbs hesitated. "All right. Move aside."

Keeping himself between the sheriff and Paris, Finn lets the sheriff up on the front porch. The sheriff muttered some ugly things under his breath, opened the door to look in, and stumbled back.

There weren't a lot of murder victims in Silver Mist.

Finn could see that it was murder right away. The blood spilled out from beneath the body was a dead giveaway. He also knew that he and Paris weren't in any danger. The violent energy around the dead body was all but dissipated.

"What happened," Dobbs demanded. "Your statements. Now."

"I found it first," Paris volunteered as she stepped forward. Finn wanted to restrain her, to keep her from the ugliness that was spilling out from the sheriff, but he kept his hands in his pocket. She obviously wanted to make an impression, and he wasn't going to step in the way of that. "I wanted to take a look around the house."

"Trespassing," Dobbs growled.

"I had a key."

"And she owns half the house," Finn said mildly.

At the way Paris snapped her head up, he could see that she didn't know. Oh, Helena really did want to cause some chaos. Dobbs actually took a step back in surprise. Or maybe it was horror. "Excuse me?"

"Helena left the house to both Paris and I, so she's not trespassing. She had every right to be here. Continue."

Paris cleared her throat. "Right, as I was saying, I

wanted to look around, so I went inside, and there was that poor man. Finn was right behind me..."

"Did you two come together? I see neither one of you parked in the driveway. Also, nice Porsche, hotshot."

"It's Finn," he said mildly. "Not hotshot. And we did not come together. I pulled up right behind Paris with the same intention. I'd been here earlier, but I only wanted to make sure that my keys worked, and then I planned to get a room at the bed and breakfast."

Dobbs grunted. "Good cause you won't be staying here until we process the scene. Do you know the man?"

"I didn't get a good look at his face," Finn said. "Paris?"

"No. I mean, I saw his face, but I didn't really look at it. It's just awful. What was he doing in there? What happened to him?"

"Well, it looks to be like he's been stabbed. As for what he was doing there, we'll determine that. As much as I hate to say this, don't leave town. We're going to have some questions for you."

PARIS STILL LOOKED like she might have been in shock, so Finn drove her back to the bed and breakfast. When they pulled into the parking lot, she turned and stared at him. "It was nice of you to make up that story about the house. But it won't take the sheriff long to figure out I don't own any part of it."

"You do," said Finn.

"What now?"

"Helena left you half the house and all of the possessions inside. The other half to me. Cash assets went to me. There was a collection of books she'd loaned the historical society that she said they could keep. That was it."

"I don't understand. The property gets passed down in the family here in Silver Cove. I was not family. We weren't even speaking to each other. I hadn't seen her in twenty years."

"Why were you in the house, Paris? Looking to reconnect with old memories somehow?"

"No." She laughed dryly. "This is going to sound so cold, but I just have this feeling there's something in the house that I need to see. It's connected...oh, never mind. I'm sure you don't care. Thanks for dropping me off here."

"I wasn't just dropping you off." Finn turned off the car and unhooked his seat belt. "I'm staying here too."

"You are? Why? You inherited the house."

There were some things he wasn't ready to tell Paris. "We inherited the house," he reminded her.

The house had redecorated itself — whether it was before Darren Jones was murdered or after, Finn couldn't tell. But the old-fashioned decor that had always been to his aunt's taste was gone. The floral wallpaper in the foyer was gone, replaced by a warm grey paint job. In place of the old slate floor were gleaming dark oak panels and a bright cream rug.

And when he'd stepped in behind Paris that night, the house had wrapped him in warm and welcoming vibes. It had wanted him there with Paris.

But she wasn't ready to hear any of that, and he wasn't prepared to explain it.

"Didn't want to spend the night until I got a good look at the place," he said mildly.

Paris blew out her breath. "That was excellent thinking. What if you'd been there when that man was killed?"

If he had been there, Paris wouldn't be wrapped up in another mystery, but Finn didn't voice that out loud.

Instead, he was wondering if it would just be better for Paris to leave town as soon as the police allowed it.

Safer for her. Isn't that what Helena had always said? Safer for Paris to stay away.

CHAPTER 5
PARIS

A major storm was brewing off the shores. From the window of her room, Paris could see lightning streaking from the sky and the boom of thunder, but as usual, there was nothing more than a light mist on the window.

Even if it hadn't been storming, Paris wouldn't have been able to sleep. She couldn't get the dead man out of her mind. Or the necklace he'd been wearing around his neck.

Green. Green monsters echoing in the dark.

Closing her eyes, she shook her head as her heartbeat sped up. It was just the stress of being back, combined with the shock of finding that poor man. It was playing with her mind.

Turning from the storm, she wrapped her arms around her body. On her bed, Sugar was curled up against the pillows and snoring loudly. The travel and abrupt move didn't bother him. Very little bothered him. Maybe that's why Paris kept him around. He was her steady little man.

Finn, on the other hand. Well, he'd been pretty steady tonight, too, hadn't he? The memory of his breath in her ear as he steered her out of the house cropped up in her mind. Her heart sped up again, but for a completely different reason.

Just because she'd seen Finn in her waking dream and again here didn't mean anything. The memory of him was connected to Helena and the memory of Silver Mist. He spent his summers with Helena, just like she did. As the older, cooler, and gorgeous teenager in town, he was a heartthrob to every female under the age of eighteen, and when he hit eighteen, well — let's just say Paris was always a little suspicious of the amount of work Mrs. Guntherson found for Finn to do.

He wasn't there that summer. She never even got to say goodbye to him. They were close, and she'd had so many dreams of him looking at her and seeing her as more than the snot-nosed kid his aunt watched. Since the moment she realized what a crush was, she'd crushed hard on Finn.

Now, they were the proud co-owners of a crime scene not exactly what she'd envisioned when she thought of seeing him again.

After a glance at the clock, she realized that she was not going to go to sleep anytime soon. If she was lucky, she'd find some tea in the kitchen to help soothe her.

Opening the door, she snuck quietly out, but when she closed the door behind her, the one across the hall opened, and Finn stepped out.

They stared at each other.

"Can't sleep?" He asked roughly.

"I was just going to go down and get some tea."

"Go back to your room. I'll bring you up a mug. Something herbal, right?"

"Yes. Were you going for tea?"

"Was thinking of something stronger, but tea might be good. I'll be back in a few minutes."

Reopening her door, she backed into her room, looked around, and panicked at how messy it was. She'd been here less than twelve hours, but it was like she'd just taken all her clothes, tossed them in the air, and let them fall where they wanted.

It wasn't quite that dramatic, but Paris had definitely made a mess while she dug around to find the perfect *I'm back, and I don't want to talk about it* outfit.

It wasn't her fault she didn't know it was also going to be, and *I found a dead body and had some strange anxiety attack* outfit, too. It was a pair of jeans and a knitted sweater. It shouldn't have had to work that hard.

With more energy than she'd had all day, she moved like a whirlwind through the room to tidy up as best she could. Sugar snoozed right through it.

Finally, there was a light knock at the door, and Paris opened it with a nervous smile. Finn was juggling a tray of mugs and a tea kettle. "Chamomile, okay? They had jasmine."

"Chamomile is great. Come in."

Finn glanced nervously inside. "Dog gonna be okay with that?"

"Sugar? Of course. He'd never hurt a fly." The dog in question was awake now and in his bread-loaf position, paws entirely tucked under his body. Paris always thought he looked so cute in that position. He was watching Finn with steady curiosity.

Just the sweetest boy. "If you sit on the bed, he might curl up in your lap."

"Uh-huh. Maybe next time."

Too late, Paris realized she'd just tried to get Finn on the bed. "Not like that, I mean. Just, Sugar likes people."

"Sure. I would have guessed that by the fury in his eyes as he tracks me across the room."

"Fury?" Paris laughed. "You're terrible at reading dogs. I'd ask what's keeping you awake, but I imagine it's the same thing as me. I keep thinking Sheriff Dobbs might call with more questions, but it's almost one o'clock in the morning. I'm sure he's not even working at this hour."

"He called me." Sitting the tray on the small round table, Finn sat in the armchair next to it and poured their tea.

Paris tried not to let her rage show. "Of course he did."

"You two seem to have a history."

Oh, they had a history all right. Dobbs was a young deputy when she, Sage, and Ginger went missing. He was the first to tell the news that they thought the young teenagers were making it up, looking to seek attention.

He'd been young, only a few years older than they were when they went missing, and over the years, when she thought about it, she tried to tell herself that he'd been young and eager to make a name for himself. Victim blaming was not the way to do it, but again, he'd been young.

Clearly, he hadn't gotten any wiser.

"What did he say?"

"Name of the victim. Darren Jones. Wanted to know if I had a history with him."

"Did you?"

"I knew him from around town. He's been here for years. Used to own a restaurant in town but retired a few years ago. Apparently, he's got a record from his early twenties. Stealing. Dobbs thinks Darren might have been in the manor to scavenge it before we arrived."

The tea burned her mouth, and Paris just cradled it while she sat on the edge of the bed. "Early twenties? He looked like he was in his fifties. That's a long time to continue stealing and not getting caught. Or to decide to start back up again."

"I agree. If he was in there to steal, he must have been looking for something in particular. Dobbs wanted to know what I thought that might be."

Paris waited for him to continue, but he just leaned back in his chair and sipped his tea thoughtfully. "Well? Did you?"

"Don't know. Aunt Helena had some valuable pieces of jewelry and some antiques that might be worth something. I won't know until I get the items appraised. Or until we get them appraised, I suppose."

We. Paris still couldn't wrap her head around the fact that Helena had left her half the house. Part of her wanted to apologize for it, but Finn didn't seem too upset about it. Maybe he knew it was coming, so it didn't surprise him.

"I don't even know where you live," she said softly. "After we lost touch. You don't live here since you're staying at the bed and breakfast."

"I don't. I have a condo about two hours away."

"Helena must have liked having you close by."

"Hard to tell what Helena liked. She wasn't the warm and fuzzy type," Finn pointed out. "Drink your tea."

The cup was cooling down, and she hadn't even realized it. Slowly, she sipped her tea and sighed as the warm liquid slid down her throat and into her belly. Something about it instantly put her at ease and made her think of curling up in bed.

She looked over the rim and found Finn studying her. His face had matured. The boyish good looks had turned downright handsome, but there was something hard about his face. His eyes were still a brilliant blue, but the dark hair that used to curl wildly down his neck was cropped short. His face was a little more angular, and his body a little harder.

Whoops. Don't think about his body, Paris. Focus. Shared assets. Dead body. *You're not a teenager anymore. Stop acting like one.*

"What do you want to do with the house? Are you thinking of moving here?"

Tipping back his cup of tea, Finn finished it and stood. He placed it on the tray and sighed. "I think, Paris, that you should let me buy out your half. You can get back to your life and away from all of this."

Oh. So much for hoping there might be some brewing chemistry happening between them. "Get some sleep," he finished. "I'll see you tomorrow."

She gave him a tight smile as he walked out. Her mind swirled again, but this time, she could put the cup down, and she was asleep before the tea cooled the rest of the way.

"Paris! Oh my goodness, it is so good to see you! Look at how beautiful you are! What in the world is that?"

Laughing, Paris put Sugar down so she could hug Annie. The elderly woman looked fantastic. She had to be in her seventies, but she honestly didn't look a day over fifty, and the man next to her was as handsome as she remembered. "This is Sugar."

"Sugar," Annie crooned and bent down to pet him, but the dog danced away and barked maniacally at her. "Oh."

"He woke up a little grumpy," Paris explained while Duke pulled out the patio chair for her. Paris sat and grinned. "You know, Duke, there's a giant picture of you hanging in the bed and breakfast lobby claiming that you're the mayor, but I just couldn't believe it."

"Oh, believe it," Duke said ruefully. "I keep trying to retire, but they keep writing my name on the ballot every year."

"Don't let him fool you. He loves it," Annie assured her.

It was inching towards noon the next day. Paris had slept in late and woken up to find that Finn was gone. Since she didn't have his number, she couldn't text him, so she spent the morning catching up on her emails and accepted a lunch date when Annie had clumsily texted her.

"Now explain to me again why you are staying at that ancient and dusty bed and breakfast when we have a perfectly good guest room for you," Annie demanded as a waitress walked out and handed them menus. Annie waved her away. "Please, I know what we're getting. Does it look like we need menus?"

"I do," Paris said as she reached out and snagged one. "I don't live here, remember? And I don't want to put you out. The B&B is great. Really."

They were at Green Brews, which was apparently now open for weekend brunch. She hadn't been here since it was Jack's Brews, back when the old wood counter still bore the scars of decades of use and the clink of beer mugs competed with music from a dusty jukebox. Now, it was all warm light, pressed herbs, and enchanted tea blends. Paris couldn't help but look around for her old friend, but she had a feeling that Sage was long gone. She'd wanted so desperately to get out of town. She was probably a model in Europe now. She'd certainly been gorgeous enough to be one.

After perusing the menu, she ordered a coffee and the eggs Benedict. Annie and Duke both ordered waffles and when the waitress was gone, Annie reached over and took her hand. "Sheriff Dobbs, of course, called us and told us about poor Darren. Imagine my shock when he said that you'd found the body!"

Paris caught them up on everything, including how Helena had left the manor to both her and Finn. "Of course, she'd do something so complicated. She always had a flair for the dramatic. She just tried to wrap it up in that homebody baker persona. I honestly hoped she would leave you the house. Finn would just sell it if it was his free and clear. He's never really had a connection to the town. Not like you did."

"Annie, you know I'm not staying. My connection to the town isn't exactly a good one."

"Pish posh. That was years ago. Nobody remembers that."

"Sheriff Dobbs does," Paris said quietly. As did all the residents who'd gone out of their way to get a look at her yesterday, but she didn't tell Annie that. It would just upset her. She was always one to look on the bright side.

Duke growled. "I'll have a word with him. Never thought he should be sheriff. Not after what he did. Luckily, I'm his boss now."

"I'm not a teenager anymore. I think I can handle Sheriff Dobbs on my own."

"Annie, Duke. I'm so sorry," a voice called from behind her. "But we're out of strawberries for the waffles. Will bananas be okay?"

With a gasp, Paris whipped her head around. Sage stood in the open door to the kitchen, and she looked just as shocked as Paris.

Green flashed in her eyes, and Paris gasped. Green monsters. Echoing in the darkness. Flashing in and out. Blinking menacingly at her.

Except that it wasn't a green monster at all. It was an amulet dancing around in her memories.

The exact amulet that Darren Jones had around his neck when he was killed in Helena's house.

CHAPTER 6

PARIS

"Paris?" Sage hesitated before giving her a small smile. "I'd heard that you were back in town."

Realizing that she was being rude, Paris got up and went to awkwardly hug her old friend. "I would have looked you up sooner, except that I didn't know you were still here."

"Ah. Yeah. I guess I had big plans, didn't I? Well, my father passed away, and Green Brews is mine, so I figured, what the hell. I guess I'm a masochist. You look good, Paris. I'd stay and chat with you more, but we're about to hit our rush."

"No, no. I understand."

"Um." Sage hesitated again. "How long are you staying in town?"

A minute ago, Paris would have said not long, but the new memory had taken hold and wouldn't let go. Paris knew, without a doubt, that she couldn't leave town until she'd figured out, once and for all, what had happened to the three of them all those years ago.

It occurred to her that Sage might remember even more.

And Ginger? She had no idea where Ginger was, but it couldn't be that hard to find her.

It was finally time to piece it all together.

"A while, I think," Paris said confidently. "I can give you my phone number, and you can let me know when might be a good time for us to get together and catch up."

"Perfect. Write it down here." Sage passed her server pad to Paris and looked over her shoulder. "Anne? Duke? Bananas?"

"That sounds wonderful," Annie said.

At the same time, Duke shook his head. "No fruit for me, thanks. I'll just take the carbs and Sugar."

Scowling, Annie poked at him and sighed. Paris scribbled her number down and passed it back to Sage. From the way her old friend was looking at her, Paris figured there was about a thirty percent chance she might not hear from her.

"I'm so sorry, Paris," said Annie in an exaggerated whisper. "I should have known you didn't realize Sage was here. I think I just assumed that you three girls kept in touch. You were so close. You know, when you were all turning double digits, there was a town meeting about the amount of trouble you three were getting into. That was the summer you tried to dye the koi pond pink."

Unable to help herself, Paris laughed. "I remember that. We were really into pink that summer. I think we also painted Sage's front door pink. Her father was not a fan."

"I imagine not," Duke said dryly.

"When did he pass away?" Paris felt some guilt that she hadn't known.

"Not long. Maybe two years ago. He'd been ill for a long time, but he refused to go in for testing. Never did trust doctors. Sage nearly worked herself to the bone trying to keep the bar running and take care of her father."

"That's terrible. I wish, well, I wish so many things had been different."

Making a noise, Annie reached across and took her hand. "I wish I could speak for the whole town, but I know a lot of people regret how they acted, what they said. It was just so terrifying for everyone, and they all forgot how terrifying it must have been for you. I know you don't want to talk about it, but if being here brings up any bad memories or feelings, I do hope you'll let me know."

"I appreciate that. What do you know about Ginger?"

"The last time I saw her was at her mother's funeral. That was...a little over ten years ago, I suppose. She had the most darling little girl with her. Oh, I wish I could remember her name, but my mind isn't what it used to be. I guess after her mother was gone, there was no need for Ginger to return. We haven't seen her since. Her little girl must be all grown up. A teenager now."

Annie smiled wistfully. Paris wondered if she and Duke ever regretted not having children. She didn't know much about their marriage. Now, it seemed the two decades in age that separated them wasn't much, but when she was younger, Annie and Duke had always seemed *old*.

They chatted a little bit more over brunch, and Paris found herself laughing more than she had in ages. There was something cathartic in being with Annie and Duke and connecting to the town again.

There was also something cathartic about the decision she'd made, and she couldn't wait to get started.

That night, she was going to break the law.

. . .

Reparations were his wheelhouse, but only when it came to the natural elements. So when Finn cut through the sheriff's department's seal on the door, he hoped that the house would help hide his tracks. Closing the door, he placed his hand on the other side. "Help out an old friend, would you?" he murmured.

The smooth wood tingled under his hands. Finn couldn't check that the crime tape was resealed without opening the door, but he had a feeling that the house was on his side.

It was probably better to seal it after he left and not waste the house's magic twice, but he wasn't sure how long he would be there, and he didn't know if Dobbs would put a guard at the door. Unlikely, this late at night, especially if there wasn't one already, but he couldn't risk it.

He wasn't sure what he was doing back here except that the body of Darren had spooked Paris. More than "*Is that a dead body?*" kind of spooked.

He hadn't lied to her exactly. Just withheld some of the truth. If Helena was right, then this town was dangerous for her, and Paris, at least the Paris that he remembered, would dig her heels in and insist on helping with the investigation until she learned the truth if given half a chance.

In fact, the only time Paris had given up was when she'd been run out of town.

She'd just been a kid. Finn would never forgive Silver Mist for that.

Maybe, just maybe, the house would tell him what happened, and he could put the matter to rest before Paris got hurt.

He and the house hadn't always gotten along. Growing up in a magical family, but with minimal magical abilities, hadn't been easy. He was supposed to train with Helena,

45

much like Paris, but Helena was never interested in training Finn. Helena has preferred to focus on Paris even though she showed no signs of unlocking her magic.

And the house, well, the manor, always seemed to have magic to spare. For a surly teenager, it was a hit to his ego.

As an adult, he and the house had come to some sort of compromise. It would quit doing its hijinks, like stealing his electric razor and hiding it in the refrigerator, and he would quit sucking up its magic and blowing it on silly things like turning the backyard into a massively overgrown jungle.

Helena had not appreciated that joke.

Now that the house half belonged to him, he wasn't sure where they stood. On the one hand, it had decided to magically redecorate, and it was certainly much more to his taste.

Of course, it hadn't redecorated until after Paris had gotten into town, so apparently, it was still going to try to be a little difficult.

"You can't belong to the both of us, you know. Helena was trying to stir up trouble, but this is the real world. I'll buy out her half."

The wall color darkened a little bit, and Finn sighed. "For now, how about we focus on the dead body on the floor? You got anything to say about that?"

Silence. So silent, in fact, that Finn could hear the tell-tale sound of plastic rippling just outside the front door. Immediately, he stepped through the doorway on the left, which led into a sitting area, and pressed his back against the wall.

Sure enough, the door opened tentatively.

At first, there was nothing. Then, the tippy-tapped sound of nails hitting the wood.

"No," he growled as he walked back out into the foyer.

Paris shrieked, bent down, and snatched up Sugar. "No. You are not breaking into the house, and you are definitely not doing it with a chihuahua. Go, and we can both pretend this never happened."

Her eyes narrowed dangerously, and she thrust out her chin. "I have as much right to be here as you do."

"Which, at the moment, is no right at all. Why don't you leave the trespassing of crime scenes to me."

"What, are you going to pat me on the head and call me a little lady?" Rolling her eyes, she put Sugar down and closed the door the rest of the way behind her.

Taking a deep breath, he counted to ten. "No, I'm not. I'm just trying to protect you, Paris."

"Yeah. I guess it'll be hard for me to leave town if I'm in jail, huh."

Oh. So she wasn't taking that well. "What are you here for?"

"Same as you, I expect. I'd like some answers about Mr. Darren Jones."

There was a new, no-nonsense tone in her voice. It was vastly different than the tone of voice she was using last night. "Have you come across some information that you'd like to share with me?"

"No. Maybe. Okay, fine. I think he was the guy who kidnapped me and my friends. And before you say that my mind is just playing tricks on me being back in town, you should know that my mind has been playing tricks on me since I *left* town. Recognizing the amulet around his neck is the first thing that has made sense to me about those missing nights. I'm not wrong. He was involved somehow, or he got his hands on an amulet that belonged to someone else."

"The amulet is his. I've never seen him without it." He

didn't bother asking Paris if she was sure. It was obvious that she was. "What do you mean your mind has been playing tricks on you?"

She opened her mouth and then clamped it shut, eyes going wide. Paris would be the world's worst poker player. Just like when she was younger, she wore all her emotions right there on her face. It was obvious she'd realized she'd made a big mistake.

"It's okay, Paris. No judgments here. I'm not going to assume that you've gone crazy. You clearly went through a trauma that you can't remember. Your mind is going to process that somehow, even now, after all this time."

"What are you, a therapist?" She muttered and sighed. "Fine. I get these very vivid dreams. Right before I found out that Helena had died, I had this waking dream."

"A vision?"

"Well, no. Visions aren't real, right? This was just...it was the town covered in heavy black smoke. I could see you and me at the B&B. And Helena was telling me to return. The first time she'd spoken to me since I left."

Finn's heart dropped. "Smoke. Like, a fire?"

"No, I don't think so. It was different, but I can't explain why."

He knew what that was, and it was no waking dream. Helena had the power of telepathy. She could send images and vocal messages. It made things hard when he was a young boy and teenager trying to be cool, and his aunt was asking in his mind if he'd done laundry in the last month.

"When was this exactly."

"Day before I arrived."

Helena was already dead then, which meant she'd found a way to reach Paris from beyond the grave. And the only way she could have connected with her, dead or alive, was if Paris had magic.

That didn't make any sense. Paris's parents were both magical but had shunned their magic. When Paris was born, they decided it wasn't fair to make the same decision for their child. So, when she was old enough to start manifesting her magic, they sent her to Helena, who'd been part of their parent's coven, to give her a chance to grow her magic with Helena as a tutor.

Only Paris's magic had never manifested. Finn had assumed that Paris was human, having managed to dodge inheriting any magical gifts. He knew that Helena thought differently, or at least had hoped differently.

She is meant for great things.

Then Paris had left, and the time for her magic to show itself had passed. There had no longer been any danger of it triggering, and now she was in her forties.

"Paris, do you ever look down the street and think people look...different to you?"

"What do you mean? Everyone is different. It'd be weird if I looked around and thought everyone was the same."

"No, not from each other. From what you know them to be."

"Uh, no? That's a weird question."

"Sorry. I know. Listen, when you have these dreams, are they about random things? Or something specific."

She glanced away from his and studied the floor. "They're about those nights, okay? They don't make sense. There are no real memories coming forth. I'm just a teenager reliving those nights. They don't make sense."

"But you associated your waking dream with it even though it wasn't about those nights. Were you and I teenagers when you saw us in your vision?"

Paris blinked and stared at him. "No," she whispered. "No, we were in the present."

Finn's heart dropped. In addition to being a telepath, Helena could occasionally see the future. Powerful visions. It wasn't magic specific to her bloodline but rather to what her role was in town. It was that magic that allowed her to see the future.

She'd tried to send Paris a vision. Paris, who didn't believe in magic. Paris, who wasn't supposed to be magical.

The ground below them rumbled, and a picture fell from the wall and shattered. "Earthquake," Paris gasped. Finn grabbed her by the arms and pushed her up against the doorway, covering her body with his own. The rumbling grew more intense and lasted what seemed like minutes.

In reality, it was only it was seconds.

When it finally stopped, he pulled away. "Paris, are you all right?"

She opened her eyes. They were a vibrant purple swirling with pinks and silvers. It was like looking into a mystical galaxy. *"The guardians are here,"* she roared. Magic ripped out of her, and she clung to him. *"The witch. The fey. The human. They are mine, and I am theirs once again."*

Finn swore, and Paris's eyes closed. When they opened again, she looked at him with confusion. "Wow. I didn't even know Silver Mist Cove could get earthquakes."

They couldn't, but Finn didn't tell her that. With all the magic that was wafting off her, Finn knew that in due time, she'd be demanding answers.

And he'd do what no one else had. He'd finally tell her the truth.

CHAPTER 7

???

Magic drenched the town as the Ley line finished with its overdramatic performance. A figure stood at the darkened window that looked to the forest as the building came to rest.

The last guardian had arrived.

A cold fury stirred in his chest. A plan that had been years in the making should have taken only an hour to perform, and yet here he was, twenty-five years later, still trying to complete it.

Who would have guessed that an inept witch, an ignored fey, and a pathetic human would have stopped him? Mere teenagers.

What a horrid mistake he'd made then. Killing them would have been easier. Quicker. Instead, a town that built its roots on protecting people turned against them, ran them off, and he'd had to wait.

Months turned into years turned into decades. He'd moved carefully. Whispered in the right ears. Tugged on the right heartstrings. All that he could do, discreetly, was to get the wayward guardians back into town so the ley line would open back up again.

Patience. Oh, it had taken so much patience. Then, when it finally looked like the stars had aligned, one swift spell took out the old guardian.

Killing a witch as powerful as Helena had not been easy. He'd taken a risk. If he had hesitated for even a moment, he'd be dead, and the lion that was the guardian of the town's magic would know the truth.

He was smart, though. Powerful. What would his family think now if they could see him?

Closing his eyes, he let the magic wash over him, the magic he hadn't felt in years. Like many of the residents, he breathed it in and basked in it. Did the idiots in Silver Mist know that their actions had chased away much of their magic, too? That running those girls out of town had reper-cussions.

He hoped they did. What they'd done was reprehensi-ble. He hoped they'd connect the dots and realize they had only themselves to blame.

As for the women, well, they deserved their accolades. They deserved to see the town throw themselves at their mercy and beg for forgiveness.

Maybe, if he had time, he'd let them have that. But Silver Mist was never one to fall on their knees for anything, and he'd waited long enough.

No, there would be no accolades. No rituals in their honor. He would be powerful, but he was not patient.

The ley line was awake and at its most vulnerable. It reached for its guardians, seeking the protection it had for centuries.

But the guardians would not be reaching back. They

had no idea what they were. And if he moved swiftly enough, then they would never know.

Finally, the magic of Silver Mist Cove would be his.

CHAPTER 8
PARIS

The Uber driver was ten feet tall.

Paris, leash in hand, stopped her walk short and stared as the driver got out of his vehicle and opened the trunk. A young man got out of the back seat, grabbed his guitar, and thanked the creature before heading toward an apartment complex.

Tall was one thing. Six feet tall was fine. Nice even. Especially if it had the whole yummy, tall, dark, and handsome vibes to go with it, Finn was a little over six feet. He also had the whole tall, dark, and handsome vibe.

Seven feet was unusual. Paris would definitely take a second look at seven feet, maybe even have the urge to comment on it, but think better of it because a person who was seven feet tall would hear comments like that their whole lives.

The driver was not seven feet tall.

Maybe ten feet tall was an exaggeration. Paris couldn't say exactly how tall the driver was, but he definitely stretched when he got out of the car.

And then shrank when he got back into it.

Shrank.

People could hunch. Fold themselves up, even. Seeing large people in small cars could be comical that way.

But people did not shrink. Paris was very firm on that.

As the Uber pulled away, Paris tried to remember when the last time was that she had eaten. After the earthquake, Finn had hustled her home. Something about Dobbs might be needing to check on the crime scene afterward.

He also mentioned Paris not trespassing alone. The way he phrased it was encouraging. Not that she couldn't do it, but that she shouldn't do it alone.

He also mentioned leaving the dog at home when committing crimes. She would ignore that piece of advice. Sugar was an asset.

She hadn't had dinner before the earthquake, so brunch was her last meal. That was over twelve hours ago. Clearly, she was having some kind of sugar crash.

"We'll check out the kitchen when we head back in. See if we can't come up with something to eat before we go to bed," Paris told Sugar and turned back to the bed and breakfast. They'd only walked a few blocks. Paris had hoped to walk a few more. Exercise was key for the tubby chihuahua. And less cookies, although Paris struggled with that.

Wings.

Paris stopped short again and stared at a couple exiting the apartment building. They both had wings.

Just a costume. A really good costume, Paris told herself. Except...was that some kind of glitter coming off the wings? Like fairy dust.

Paris, do you ever look down the street and think people look...different to you?

It was an odd question then, but now? Paris tore her

gaze from the couple, snatched up Sugar, and raced down the street toward Rose's.

Thankfully, there were still no other guests in the building, or someone might have objected to the way that Paris pounded on Finn's door. It barely opened before she threw herself inside.

"What? What's wrong?" Finn stared out the door as if he expected someone to be chasing her.

"You...are not wearing a shirt."

Slowly, Finn closed the door and turned. He was still wearing the jeans he had on earlier, but only that. His bare chest was, well, it was nice if Paris was going to have an opinion about it, but also, the fact that his feet were bare just made the whole scene seem even hotter.

Was he getting ready for bed? If she'd waited just a few more minutes...

"Focus, Paris. I doubt you flew into my room because you suspected I was undressing." He paused. "I know how that sounded, and it was not how it was meant to sound."

"Yes. Focus. There are fairies in Silver Mist."

"Fairies," he commented.

"Uh-huh. They're definitely bigger than I imagined they would be, but they have wings and fairy dust wafting off them. Also, I think the local Uber driver might be part giant. Maybe small for a giant, but definitely too big to be human. At first, I thought, sugar crash. I hadn't eaten in a while. Burned off some energy breaking and entering into a crime scene and then being in the middle of an earthquake." And being in his arms. "But then, I remembered what you said."

"Good."

"I remembered what you said about did I see things that appear to be different. First, I thought you maybe meant purple hair and black lipstick kind of different."

"I meant magical creatures."

"But you strike me as the progressive type. Not that I think purple hair and black lipstick are progressive. People should wear what makes them happy, and it shouldn't be a statement."

"You are correct."

Paris stopped her rant. "You said magical creatures."

"Paris, you should sit down, but before you do that, maybe you could grab your dog before he pees on my leg."

"Sugar! Oh, he's just sniffing. He would never potty indoors." Paris grabbed the dog and sat neatly in the armchair. "Okay. I'm listening."

And she was. There were any number of explanations for what was happening here. Drugs were the expected answer. Finn had said that he was a business consultant, but maybe that was a lie, and he was an undercover DEA agent.

Or maybe the earthquake had released some kind of noxious gas. Maybe Finn was a geologist who was studying the area for some strange phenomenon.

"You're a witch."

"No," Paris answered calmly. "You can tell me the truth, Finn."

"I am. Paris, the reason you came to Silver Mist Cove every summer was because your parents were witches. I don't know all the details. Only what Helena had explained to me, she was a friend of your grandparents. Magic runs in your family; only your parents decided not to practice. They would not, however, make that decision for you, so they sent you here so you could decide for yourself what to do. Everyone was waiting for your magic to manifest so she could teach you."

Paris frowned. It was a lot of information, and she

decided to take a little bit at a time. "My father was a school teacher, and my mother was a sociologist. I came to town so they could travel in the summer for my mother's research."

"They could have taken you with them. Given both of your parent's professions, I think they would have jumped at the chance to have a daughter who was well-traveled, don't you think?"

Oh. Well, yes.

"Helena never talked about magic. She never tried to teach me to cast spells."

"Your magic never manifested. At least, that's what we all thought. Except that Helena communicated with you from beyond the grave, so somehow, that's not true. You must have had your magic all along. Maybe you couldn't manifest it for some reason?" He started muttering to himself and pacing. "But I think that's something Helena would have been able to see it. I mean, I can see your magic now, and I'm not much of a witch. You're practically glowing."

"I'm glowing?" Paris stared down at herself. "You have magic?"

"Helena was my aunt by blood. My mother was her sister. They were both witches. Powerful ones, but my father is human. Helena always hated that my mother married a human."

Her temples started to throb. "Finn, you're not a witch. Sage, Ginger, and I used to follow you to the beach to watch you swim. You never did anything magical."

"You did what?"

Oops. "Sorry. We were kids. We stopped doing it when we were teenagers." Seventeen counted as a teenager, right?

"I used to swim naked."

"I closed my eyes during that part, but I don't think Sage did."

"We're going to table that for now, but we are definitely going to circle back to it. I didn't perform any water magic, so you wouldn't have seen me do any magic at the beach. In fact, I didn't perform much magic at all when you were here. Helena's orders. It was easy enough since you were here during the tourist season. All the locals cap their magic during tourist season. Most children don't learn what their parents are until they're old enough to handle it in front of strangers. I think Sage learned about her father right after you left."

"Sage is a witch?"

"Sage is fey. She's the daughter of the Green Man."

Fey. Fairies. This was getting ridiculous. "Finn, I'm going to go down to the kitchen, get some food, and go to bed. I think I'm having one of those waking dreams I was telling you about."

"So nice of you to inform the dream version of me what you're planning on doing," Finn sighed. "Come back when you've slept. I think it's important that you know the truth."

"Sure. I'll do that."

He didn't stop her as she left. She deposited Sugar in her room and went down to the kitchen. Normally, Rose didn't allow guests to wander in and out, but since it was her and Finn, locals, she didn't go all out for meals and just told them they were welcome to whatever they wanted.

It mainly was stocked with basics. She'd eat a bowl or two of cereal, just something to take the edge off and go to bed. Things would be back to normal in the morning.

An hour later, she politely knocked on Finn's door. This

time, when he opened it, he had a shirt on. She barely registered her disappointment before he pulled her inside.

"Sorry, I don't know how to do this without you thinking you're hallucinating, but maybe if I show you some of my magic, you'll understand. My family is strongly connected to the earth's elements, although my magic manifests better at night. Helena thinks there might be a lunar witch in our family. In any case, just sit down and watch."

"That's not necessary," Paris started as she sat, but Finn waved his hand.

"No, it is necessary. Magic is personal, and I should not have been the one to tell you. It should have been your parents. Or Helena. It doesn't feel right to tell you who you are without me showing you who I am. This is Fig."

He held out a small potted succulent of some kind. "He's about twenty years old."

"Wow. I didn't know succulents lived that long."

"It varies from species to species, but yes. This is a short-lived grocery story succulent. It's lived this long because I've connected with it, a little bit like a familiar. I feed him magic, and he manipulates it and feeds it back to me. Earth is not just a single element. It's complex. Fig helps me connect to different types of earth. Just watch."

He whispered to Fig, and maybe it was her imagination, but the plant seemed to sigh, and then a small tendril started to rise from the middle of the plant. It grew, thickened, and began to sprout thorns. Then, when it was about a foot and a half high, it blossomed right before her eyes, turned a brilliant red, and opened into a gorgeous rose.

"Holy crap. You just grew a long-stemmed rose from a succulent plant."

Finn frowned. "It was supposed to be a dandelion. Fig's

apparently hard of hearing today. It doesn't matter. This is me. This is part of what I can do."

"It's beautiful, Finn." Paris smiled. It was beautiful. Being able to connect to the earth was amazing. "But what I came in here to tell you was that I believe you. Rose took one look at me and turned pink. Not that I am embarrassed or getting a little angry pink, but neon pink with matching irises. Then told me that the ley line must have unlocked my magic. I decided that I wasn't hallucinating after all."

"Why not?" Finn asked warily.

"Because everything in my body pulsed like it was connected to something. I think Rose is right. Whatever a ley line is, it unlocked my magic. I feel incredible."

CHAPTER 9
PARIS

It was an entirely different world. Paris walked along the early morning streets, trying desperately not to stare at everyone she saw. Most were human, or at least looked human. Were they also hiding magic? Were witches even considered human?

Finn had explained that the town used to have a small werewolf population. It dispersed more and more as the tourist season grew bigger and bigger, but there were still a few here and there.

And dispersed among the tourists every year was a considerable number of magical creatures that all traveled to Silver Mist for one reason and one reason alone.

Beneath the town was the most extensive magical ley line in America. A natural magic conduit so powerful that it changed weather patterns, enhanced abilities, and, the one reason why there were so many fey in town, helped bolster natural glamour abilities.

It was incredible. Kids, and maybe even adults in their twenties, might wonder what lies beyond what they could see. Fantasize about getting their Hogwarts letter or becoming the chosen one.

That faded into nonsense. Here she was, forty-two years old and just coming into her witch magic. It seemed almost like a cosmic injustice, but for the first time in her entire life, she felt right.

A weight had lifted from her shoulders, and Paris wondered, if she lifted her hands toward the sky, if she might be able to fly. She felt that light.

If anyone noticed her staring, no one said anything about it.

When she wasn't staring at people, her mind was going a mile a minute. Her parents were witches. Was there any indication of their magic that she'd seen but just dismissed? Quiet arguments that she might have overheard about their decision to toss away their magic?

And why? Why would anyone give up something like this? It was intoxicating to finally understand herself. Why had her parents denied this part of themselves?

There was never a time when she didn't remember them being happy, though. While the decision they had made for themselves was hard for her to understand, it had seemed to make them happy. And obviously, they hadn't tried to make the same decision for her.

Still, her mother died two years ago. *Two years ago.* In all that time, she'd never once mentioned magic or witchcraft.

And Helena was supposed to be her teacher. Not one mention of magic. How had she spent months that accumulated to years living in a woman's house and never guessed that she was a witch?

So many secrets, and Paris had a feeling she was just beginning to peel through the layers.

"Hey."

Paris stopped short at the familiar voice and realized she'd wandered in front of Green Brews. It seemed far too early for the bar to be open, but there was Sage standing in front of the door, keys in her hand.

And Sage was green.

Not entirely green. Her skin, which had always been olive-tinted and so smooth it seemed impossible, had taken on some glowing golden hues. Soft green vines entangled with her long black, and small yellow and pink flowers peeked out from the curls. When Sage noticed Paris studying her, her eyes flashed an impossible, brilliant green.

"You can see me," Sage whispered. "Crap."

Hurriedly, she shoved the key in the door, turned it, and pulled it open. "Get inside. Quick."

Paris just stared at her friend, dumbfounded. "How?"

"Not here." Leaning forward, Sage grabbed Paris's arm and pulled her into the bar. Quickly, she locked the door behind her and blew out her breath. "This is really the kind of conversation you should have over whisky, but I guess it's a little early for that. I'm going to make some coffee. Do you want some?"

"You're fey," Paris said dumbly, still trying to process. "We were friends. Best friends. For years. How could you keep this from me?"

"Easy. I didn't know. Sit down, Paris, before you fall over. Seeing as how you saw me yesterday and didn't have this kind of reaction, I'm guessing this is a recent development. I remember how it felt to learn the truth, too. It wasn't easy. Sit here. Process the information. I'll be back with the coffee."

Finn had mentioned that a lot of the kids that grew up here didn't know what they were until they were adults. So, at least Sage hadn't kept secrets from her. That helped ease the sting a little bit.

By the time Sage returned, Paris had pulled herself together. She accepted the cup quietly, and they sipped at the hot liquid in silence before Sage nodded. "All right. So I know after the earthquake, the ley line flooded the town with magic. I don't know how it was before the line closed up, but I can tell you how it feels now. It used to be a struggle to keep the glamour in place, especially when I was angry, and believe me, working in customer service can really make a woman angry, but today, I only have to think about being human, and voila, the vines were gone."

"Not for me. They're beautiful."

"They're a pain when it comes to showering and brushing my hair. Unfortunately, fey magic doesn't mean tangle-free hair. I'm guessing the ley line unlocked your magic?"

"Did you know I was a witch?"

"Not a clue. A couple of years ago, Helena wandered into the bar. It was one of the few times that my father was feeling himself, so he was behind the bar. One look at her, and he practically threw everyone out. Myself included, only I didn't leave. It was your birthday, and she was struggling."

"She didn't reach out."

"That doesn't surprise me. She told my father you were better off gone. Safer. She said if you returned, your magic might too, and you weren't ready."

Paris frowned and cradled the cup, letting the warmth comfort her. "Returning magic implies that I had it at some point and lost it. I think I would remember that."

"Maybe. Unfortunately, that's all I got out of the conversation. I asked my father about it later, and he just gave me one of his cryptic *all will be revealed in time* crap. The man was a century old, and sometimes he forgot that this generation doesn't run on legends and myths."

"A century old," Paris squeaked. "Are you going to live that long?"

Sage twisted her lips. "I don't know. I try not to think about it that often."

"What was he? Wait, is that rude to ask? I'm so sorry. That's probably extremely rude to ask."

Laughing softly, Sage lifted her coffee and sipped from it. "Yes. I think, in general, it's a rude question to ask, but, well, given what we were and the situation, I guess it's okay to ask. My father was the Green Man."

Paris realized that Sage was waiting for a reaction, and she gave her an apologetic look. "I'm sorry. I don't really know much about the fey. Okay, I don't know anything about them."

"It's all right. It's refreshing to find someone who doesn't know who he is. Or was. In most modern retellings, the green man is an idea or, to some even, a deity. Symbolizing rebirth. But in reality, he was part of a race of fey. For the last century, he was the last of his kind."

"Are you a green man? Green woman?"

"The fey don't reproduce easily. I'm a hybrid, although I don't know anything about my mother."

"Do you have magic?"

"Not really. I'm stronger than most humans, and sometimes, if I focus hard enough, I can produce a little magic when I sing. My father once said he'd forgotten his magic, so I don't even know what he could do."

Paris's heart went out to Sage. She knew what it was like to lose a father. "I remember how protective he was of you. How much he loved you."

"The fey are like that with their children," Sage said with a sad smile. "I was so angry with him when he told me the truth. It was the summer after you and Ginger were gone. I was still angry at the world. Young and impulsive. I had a hard time settling down, and he decided it was time to tell me the truth. He removed my glamour, and I could see the town for what it really was."

"Did you feel free?"

"Free?" Sage scoffed and wrinkled her nose. "Hardly. It just made me more angry. Here was a town filled with magic that the majority of people would never know, and still they looked at what happened to us, whatever happened to us, and couldn't believe it. I was furious. I left the day after he told me. I stayed away for a whole month before someone called me to say that the bar hadn't been open in a week. That's when I realized he was sick."

"It's not easy," Paris murmured, her memories flashing back to her mother. "You stayed even after he was gone."

"I did, maybe partly because people wanted me to leave. Maybe partly because I didn't want to see the Green Brew die. In any case, I'm still here. One of those lying little girls who nearly killed the town for attention. Never mind that we were practically adults," she said sourly.

"I'm staying, Sage. What happened to us has to do with magic. I've had these flashing visions ever since I left Silver Mist. Memories that seemed more nightmare than real, but parts of them have to be real. And the dead body I found? Darren Jones? I know he was involved. I recognized his amulet. I'm going to find out what happened to us."

"Oh, Paris, I wish you wouldn't."

Of all the reactions she expected Sage to have, that wasn't one of them. Her excitement deflated, and she sat back and stared at her old friend. "You don't want to know?"

"Business is good. I feel like I'm finally breaking free of the stigma, and you're just going to stir it all up again. It's in the past, and I want it to stay there."

Shaking her head, she stood. "I'm sorry, Sage, but I can't do that. You've known who you are for twenty years now, but I'm just learning. And part of figuring all that out means I have to know what happened to us. I won't involve you, not if you don't want, but I won't stop."

"Just don't involve me. I don't want anything to do with it."

Sad, Paris nodded. She wanted Sage's help. More than that, she craved the kind of friendship they once had. Sage and Ginger were never far from her mind. There was a time when they never thought they would be a part.

But she couldn't relate to how Sage was feeling. Once Paris left Silver Mist, no one said anything to her about the event. Her parents never talked about it. Nobody else knew about it. It was like it never happened.

Sage hadn't had that luxury. Paris could see why Sage would want to distance herself.

There were some things that, apparently, even magic couldn't fix.

CHAPTER 10
FINN

This was the Silver Mist Cove he hadn't experienced in decades. The day was alive with creatures playing out in the streets and laughing like they were kids again. Everyone could feel the magic. For Finn, it was the soft tendrils of the earth reaching up to play with him wherever he walked.

Soon, the shock of it would fade. The magic would seep back down in the ley line, where it was supposed to be, and life would return to normal, but for now, the town was lit up like a block party.

When he stepped outside, fairy creatures floated by him, close enough to the ground that it would be like the trick of the light to anyone who wasn't magic. Their soft chuckles followed in their wake. Finn turned in their wake of magic and caught something as it flew into his arms.

Paris.

"This is absolutely amazing," she sighed as she wrapped her arms around his neck and stared at him. "Tell me you feel it."

She was talking about the magic, of course, but all he

could do was stare at her lips and wonder what she would do if he kissed her.

For so long, he'd wanted to taste those lips, feel her in his arms. Now, sadly, he disengaged. With this kind of magic, it would be like she was drunk for the first time. Everyone relished in the magic. Most people were able to filter it properly.

Paris was not most people.

"I feel it. Did Sheriff Dobbs call you today?"

Wrinkling her nose, she waved her hands at him. "I don't want to talk about him right now. Such a mood killer. I saw Sage. I mean, Finn, I saw Sage for the first time. She's incredible. Beautiful. Do I look different to you?"

"You're always beautiful, Paris."

She sighed longingly. "But I'm not glowy. That's all right. I haven't seen you all day. What have you been doing?"

"Taking care of a few things. I was just about to go get dinner."

"Oh! Dinner! That sounds amazing. I need to take Sugar for a walk, and then I can join you." She stopped, hesitant. "That wasn't an invitation, was it? You were just letting me know what you were doing. I'm sorry. I feel almost like I'm high right now. And even when I come down and remember that my feet are on the ground and it's all real, I still just feel incredible. Like I'm finally who I've always meant to be."

"I'm glad to hear it, Paris." He took a moment to appreciate the way she looked at the sunset. She might not think she glowed, but she was so wrong. "And you are welcome to join me for dinner."

"Great. Give me just one minute."

One minute turned into two. Then three. Finn stuck his hands in his pocket and leaned against the light post.

"What do you mean you're kicking us out?"

Paris's outraged voice carried as the door opened, and a staff member hastily left. Spinning around, Finn caught the door just as it was about to close. Paris stood at the desk, Sugar clutched in her arms.

"Paris, I'm sorry, but our pet policy clearly states that dogs need to be crated when the owner is away. Our house-keeper went in to change the sheets, and she said Sugar charged at her like a demon from the darkness. Mrs. Merry-weather is not a young woman. She has a heart condition."

"I asked for the pet policy when I checked in. Your granddaughter didn't say anything about a crate!"

"It's in the booklet of information in your room. Now, thankfully, your dog didn't bite anyone..."

"Of course, he didn't! He's very well-behaved!"

Finn cleared his throat and decided to intervene before Paris, and Sugar got into even more trouble. As usual, Sugar caught sight of him and bared his teeth. At least, what little teeth he had left.

"Paris, what I was trying to tell you earlier is that Sheriff Dobbs cleared the manor. You can check out here and move in there, temporarily, until your business is concluded. I was thinking of doing the same, but I can stay here if it would make you more comfortable."

"No," Paris all but growled. "You do not have to stay here if you don't want to. Rose, I will be packing my things immediately."

Relief swept over Rose's face, and Finn tried to hide a laugh. He didn't know if there was a crate policy or not, but Sugar was a menace, and it was obvious to everyone except his doting mother.

Since Sugar wasn't welcome back in the bed and breakfast, Finn found himself standing on the sidewalk having a staring contest with the little gremlin at the end of the leash. Occasionally, Sugar would look away, pretend to sniff something, and Finn would relax. A second later, Sugar would be right at the hem of jeans, growling menacingly.

He learned not to let his guard down.

Finally, Paris came out with her bags. "I am so sorry about all of this. You must be starving. Let me buy you dinner for helping me."

The last thing Finn wanted to do was sit on the patio with Sugar in his cranky phase. Or was this a normal phase? He was too afraid to ask. "Why don't we get settled at the manor and order a pizza?"

Her eyes lit up with delight. "That sounds perfect."

An hour later, they were lounging on the couch with an extra large pizza between the two of them. "I can't believe Mrs. Merryweather is still working for Rose. She's got to be like a hundred and twenty. Wait, is she fey too? I've got a lot of catching up to do."

"Huh. If she is fey, she keeps her glamour up all the time."

Paris bit into the pizza and tucked her feet under her. She glanced around the room and frowned. "Helena really changed her taste. I like it, and that's surprising because our tastes were never the same."

"This isn't Helena's manor."

"What? It's been a while, but I do remember the house, Finn."

"That's not what I meant. The house has some opinions it likes to express from time to time. It redecorated itself for us. Probably a blend of both our tastes."

Eyes wide, Paris stood and glanced around. "House? Are you listening to me?"

Nothing happened. Finn cleared his throat. "I don't think it responds to anything but manor."

"Oh. Right. Manor, are you listening to me? Close a door if you can hear me."

Nothing happened, and Finn couldn't help it. He started to laugh. Paris wrinkled her nose, grabbed a pillow, and threw it at him. "That's not funny."

"For all I know, the house was going to close a door. The truth is that I don't think the house is sentient. It just comes alive from time to time. You'll get used to it."

"Until I sell you my half and leave?"

That was what he'd told her. Uncomfortable, he polished off his slice of pizza and stood. "For now, we need to work on your magic. This is a much better spot than the bed and breakfast, anyway. Safer. The manor will help contain any wayward magic spills, and I'm sure there will be quite a bit. You've got a lot to learn and not a lot of time to learn it."

"Will I still have magic outside the town?"

"Of course, but I'm not saying you need to learn everything before you leave."

"Then what?"

What? That was a good question. He still needed to tell her what Helena expected of her, and he wasn't ready for that. He was sure she wasn't ready for it either.

"Let's find Helena's grimoire. That's a good place to start."

"Grimoire? That brings up some questions. How did Helena practice witchcraft all those years without me knowing? How did she hide it? Is there some secret room in the house that I don't know about it?"

"It's the attic."

"The attic?" Paris stared at him. "You're kidding, right? The attic is filled with mold and boxes. It's not even finished."

"That's the manor at work for you. Come on. Let's see if you can see for it what it really is."

Paris followed him up the stairs and hesitated when he opened the attic door. It was large enough that, if Helena had wanted to, she could have turned it into one or even two additional bedrooms. Instead, she'd kept it a creepy and unfinished storage attic. "I don't know if you remember this, but the first summer that I was here, you told me that there were snakes and rats in the attic. And serial killers."

Finn hesitated. "Huh. I do vaguely recall that, but I was ten."

"And I was eight!"

"Right. I'm sorry about that. No snakes or rats unless Helena needed them for spells."

"What? I'm not doing that?!"

"Just a little joke, Paris. No dead or snakes in the attic. I promise." She still didn't step toward him, so Finn reached out his hand without thinking. "Come on, darling. I won't let anything bad happen to you."

Her fingers wrapped around his, and he led her up the stairs into the darkness. Flipping the light switch on, he flooded the attic with light.

The manor had done some decor work up here, too. The last time he'd seen it, it had been dark hardwood with a deep red round rug that displayed the runes. Everything was dark and a little dusty. Helena had rarely turned on the light or opened the curtains but worked from candlelight instead.

Now, the curtains were gone. Just like downstairs,

everything was light and creamy. It was carpeted with a couple of couches along the walls and china cabinets with glass doors.

All very modern.

"This was not what I was expecting. I feel more like I could host a dinner party up here instead of casting spells."

"But you like it, right?"

"I do. I was definitely expecting a large cauldron, though."

Finn pointed to the cabinet. "It's in there."

Crossing to the cabinet, Paris opened it and pulled out the cauldron. "It's like three inches tall. Is this for a baby witch?"

"Spells don't require large caldrons now." Stepping over to the bookcase, Finn perused the covers. Helena might have disguised her book as something else. Or maybe the house did. "It's not here."

Paris was still staring at the cauldron. "What's not here?"

"Helena's grimoire. It's not here. That's odd."

"Maybe the manor is hiding it." She gasped. "Oh. Or maybe whoever killed Darren took it! We do think he was here to steal something. Maybe it was the Book of Spells. I'm assuming it was pretty powerful."

"It was." Finn pulled down another book and handed it to her. "We can start with this one."

"Not the book of spells but a book of spells," she said as she read the cover. "Spells for the Bored House Witch. Helena was a bored house witch?"

"No. I shudder to think of what kind of chaos she would have caused if Helena had been bored. I don't know what the is doing here, but it's the only spell book left. Your theory is as good as any."

"Finn?" Paris put the book down. "Why isn't Helena's grimoire going to you? You are her nephew."

"I was her nephew, but you were meant to be her protege. I know she'd want you to have it, assuming we can find it."

"I am definitely going to borrow it, but I'm sure she wanted you to have it. For now, I'm going to use it to get my answers. There has to be a memory-unlocking spell."

"Memory unlocking?" Finn frowned. "You're going to investigate what happened to you, aren't you?"

"Darren was there, Finn. I know it, and I'm going to find out once and for all what happened. If I can't unlock my memory, then I'm going to get my hands on the original case files. Nobody investigated because they thought we were liars. I will investigate. I'm going to find the truth, and I'm not leaving town until I do it."

Memory unlocking spell. Finn knew a few, but none of them were safe, and he wasn't going to let her try them. She was obviously serious about investigating.

And she deserved her answers.

"Will you help me, Finn? Please?"

The candles on the table flared to life, and Paris gasped. "Did you do that?"

"No. That would be the house."

"It wants you to help me."

"It would seem so."

CHAPTER II
PARIS

F inn didn't help Paris with magic last night. In fact, in the very moment that she thought things might turn in her favor, he excused himself and left.

He was gone the next morning. There was a text simply saying that he had some things to attend and he'd be back late afternoon.

Paris did what she could to entertain herself. Walking around the manor, she did her best to fight the memories that rose, and then she decided just to let it happen.

Leaning against the door jam in the kitchen, Paris thought about how Helena had tried to teach her to bake. Paris was a disaster. Flour everywhere. Food dye spilled all over the counter. The inability to measure anything correctly.

Well, not the inability. It was more like unwillingness. Paris was impatient and inattentive. Baking requires precision.

"Like magic, Paris darling. Baking is like magic. It's a spell to bring happiness to yourself and to others. You wouldn't be so unfocused if you were casting a spell, would you?"

For a moment, Paris thought she could actually see Helena in the kitchen, admonishing her. With a gasp, she blinked, but the image disappeared, as did the voice.

Had Helena actually said that? Paris had never remembered it before.

Shaking her head, she crossed the kitchen and opened the blinds. There was a nice porch attached to the back. Helena spent quite a bit of time out there at night, sitting under the stars with a shawl pulled around her shoulders.

Candles lit. A soft smile on her face. At the time, Paris thought it had just been an old woman's sentimentality.

Witchcraft. Helena hadn't even tried to hide it from her.

Shaking her head ruefully, Paris turned when movement caught her eye. She turned and froze.

Finn. It was a strange, hazy version of Finn when he was just a lanky teenager but with that heartbreaking grin.

Suddenly, Paris felt like she was twelve years old again, staring at him with her heart hammering wildly in her chest. Adults who say that kids can't possibly understand love clearly don't remember being in love for the first time. That dizzy effect that most adults would attribute to vertigo and heart attacks.

This was the first time she'd looked at Finn and realized she was in love with him. It was such a horrifying age, on the cusp of her teen years and agonizing about whether her boobs would get any bigger or if she'd ever tame the frizz in her hair. If her period would ever come or if she'd finally get to wear her pair of platform sandals that she'd been eyeing.

And there he was. Sixteen. Handsome. Confident. Still teasing her like she was his little sister, and somehow, she'd convinced herself they were meant to be together.

A sharp bark caught her attention, and a white bullet sailed through Finn's image, dissolving him.

Instantly, the white bullet turned brown. "Sugar!" Paris gasped as the chihuahua started to roll in the mud. "Oh, no. Now look what you've done."

In dismay, she hurried down the steps and picked up the dirty, squirming canine, carefully holding him away from her. A bath was not on her agenda today, but it looked like she didn't have a choice.

Woeful howls filled the house as Paris plunked her baby into the sink and hosed him down. When he resembled a drowned rat, she rolled him up in a towel and put him in the sunshine to dry.

Guarding herself against any other memories that might take hold, she went back to her hunt for Helena's grimoire. Several hours passed when the doorbell rang.

No doubt it was someone from the town bringing by a casserole with some flimsy condolences while craning their neck to look inside where a man had died. Paris had expected a line to form around the manor as soon as she and Finn moved in, but the town was showing some restraint.

Opening the door, she plastered a bright smile on her face but froze.

"Paris. I'm so sorry. I didn't know you'd be here," Ginger said, just as confused. "Although I shouldn't be surprised."

"Ginger. You're here."

Stating the obvious. Way to go, Paris.

"Yes. I...I heard about Helena, and I wanted to stop by and stay for the funeral. I hope that's all right. I know we haven't talked in a long time, but I remember Helena fondly. She put up with a lot from us."

Paris still couldn't help but stare at Ginger. Sage was

fey. What was Ginger? Fey as well? Maybe another witch? Had she known the secrets the town was hiding all along? Did she know?

"Paris? You're just staring at me. Can you say something?"

"Sorry. I was just looking for wrinkles and grey hairs. Come here." With a big smile, Paris opened her arms and enveloped her friend in a big hug. Maybe Ginger was a witch, or maybe she was just plain human, but that didn't matter to Paris. Now that her shock had worn off, she was genuinely happy to see her other older friend.

"And you look amazing," Paris added honestly as she pulled back. It was true. Ginger's red hair had darkened over the years, but it was still such a gorgeous color to frame her creamy face. Her curves were a little more volup-tuous, and her face a little rounder, but she obviously wasn't as soft as she was when they were kids. No, her eyes were guarded, and her hug wasn't quite as open as it used to be.

"Come inside. Please."

"Oh, wow," Ginger whistled as she walked in. "The place has had a whole makeover. Did Helena do this, or did you? How long have you been back?"

"Just a few days days. I didn't return until I learned that Helena had passed away. The house was like this when I got here," Paris said honestly. She wasn't sure of the rules, but if Ginger was human, Paris suspected that she wasn't supposed to tell her about the real magic within the town. "It was the first time I've been back since...we were teenagers."

Silence fell between them, and Paris's heart broke just a little bit. "Some things have changed, of course," she said hurriedly, "but much of it is the same."

"It's okay, Paris," Ginger said quietly. "It hurts. There's regret. Believe me, I know. I came back to visit a couple of times until my mom decided to move, too. I got married. Had a kid. Never really came back. I thought of Helena a lot. She called when my mom died about ten years ago. She came to the funeral with a handful of other people from the town. It was nice to catch up. I made promises to come visit, but I never did."

"Helena came to your mother's funeral?" Paris couldn't help but feel the sharp pain of betrayal. "That's nice."

"You still have a terrible poker face," Ginger said kindly and reached for Paris's hand. "As much as we built Helena up in our minds as this unflappable matriarch figure, she made mistakes. So did we."

"You think we made a mistake by leaving?"

"No. By leaving, I met the man who would be my husband. He was a terrible husband, and he's long gone from my life, but I have Ivy, my beautiful daughter. I wouldn't trade her for anything."

"Is she here with you? I'd love to meet her."

"She is, but she's a surly teenager of sixteen, and traveling to a weird small town was not her idea of summer fun. She's still at the house."

"The house. Your mom's house?"

"We never sold it. Annie helped set me up with a real estate agent who agreed to manage the property and rent it out. No one had rented it when we moved back, so I decided just to move back in. Did I hear correctly that there was a dead body in the house?"

Paris nodded and caught Ginger up on the bare facts of the case. Since Sage knew the truth, Paris decided it was only fair to tell Ginger as well. "When I saw Darren, I had a flash of memory. About those nights, we were missing. I'm certain Darren was one of our kidnappers. I think his death is tied to what happened to us, and I'm not leaving until I find the truth. I've already talked to Sage about it. She owns the bar now, and she's not on board. I'll understand if you aren't either. I can wait until after the funeral if you'd like, so you don't have to be here for it."

"No. Absolutely not," Ginger said firmly. "I've been haunted by what happened to us, by the fact that I can't remember. I want to help, Paris, and I mean that. I think that's one of the reasons that I felt compelled to return. We deserve to know."

Relief swept over Paris. "I'm so glad you feel this way."

The back door opened. "Paris, I'm back. I brought some dinner in from town, so we can just heat it up when you're ready."

Ginger's eyes widened. "You and Finn?" She whispered. "Oh my God, did you get married?"

"What? No. We just reconnected when Helena died."

"And you're already living together? Go, Paris! It's about time you finally made your move!"

Finn entered the room, and Paris cleared her throat. "Finn, I'm sure you remember Ginger. She just stopped by to say hi and let you know she'll be at Helena's funeral. Ginger and Helena left Finn and me both the manor, so we're working through the logistics of everything. It's just easier for us to stay here and go through all of Helena's things."

"I see." Ginger hid a smile. "Finn, it's really good to see you again."

"You too, and thank you for coming. It means a lot to me," Finn said.

"I won't keep you. I have to get back to Ivy before she tries to hitchhike back to town. That little earthquake spooked her, and she's certain we're going to die while we're here."

Ginger rolled her eyes, but Paris felt a shiver of awareness roll up her spine. "You were here for the earthquake?"

"It literally happened just as soon as we crossed the town line. Nothing says welcome back like the earth moving beneath you, am I right?"

AFTER GINGER LEFT, Paris and Finn heated up the dinner and sat down at the table. It was spaghetti, breadsticks, and salad from the Silver Mist Diner. It was not really where someone would expect to get an amazing spaghetti dinner, but it was just as scrumptious as Paris remembers.

"You were speaking to the funeral director today, weren't you?" Paris asked quietly. They'd avoided discussing final arrangements or even Helena's death in any kind of detail. She was still coming to terms with it, and she had no idea how Finn felt about it. Sometimes, when something from the past came up, he'd get a faraway look.

From across the table, Finn sighed. "I was. I guess I should have told you that I'm planning her funeral. You should have a say in it if you want."

"Only if you want the help or the support. You knew her better than I did, so you know what she would want. I just don't want you to feel like you have to hide it from me. Helena and I had a difficult relationship, but the funeral isn't for her. It's for you and everyone else."

"Thanks. I appreciate that."

Their gaze caught, and her smile softened. For a half second, she thought about reaching across the table to take his hand, but suddenly, the two candles on the table flared to life. Paris squeaked and jumped. "Did you do that?"

"Ah, no."

Her eyes rounded. "Did I do that?"

Soft music began to play overhead. Romantic violins, like someone was serenading them. Paris's face turned red with mortification. Was her magic somehow sensing her feelings toward Finn and trying to manifest a more romantic atmosphere? She would never live this down.

"No, you are not going it," Finn growled and stared at the ceiling. "Manor, knock it off."

The candles remained lit, and the music only grew louder. Paris relaxed and couldn't help but giggle. "I'd actually forgotten that the house could do a little magic. You know, I had visions today. Living visions of the past, memories I didn't even remember having. Was that the house?"

"Did the memories occur here?" Paris nodded. "Probably the manor."

The music intensified, and Paris cleared her throat. "Thank you for the help today, but the music is distracting. Do you think you could turn it off?"

It was strange talking to a house, but to her surprise, the music did cease. Finn grinned. "I think it likes you."

It certainly liked the two of them together, but they ignored the candles softly dancing between the two of them as they hurried through their dinner. "Do you think you can teach me some magic tonight?"

"I think we should continue looking for the grimoire. Tomorrow."

Tomorrow. That was what he said yesterday. Paris couldn't help but feel like Finn was putting her off.

That was fine. If he didn't want to teach her magic, then she would just teach herself.

CHAPTER 12
FINN

Finn slipped out of the house again before breakfast. He left another note, promising to be back after lunch. Yesterday, he'd debated asking Paris to come with him to the funeral home to help with the arrangements, but he wasn't sure how she would feel about that. Today, he knew for sure he didn't want Paris to come.

First, he was going to the mayor's house to ask if Annie had any idea where Helena's missing grimoire might be. Annie had always been an active participant in Helena's coven and one of Helena's best friends. If anyone knew, it was her. He didn't want Paris to come because not only was Annie an excellent source of information, she was a terrible gossip.

Soon, everyone would know that he and Paris were both staying at the manor. The more things they did together, the more rumors would fly, and he wanted to shield Paris from that as much as possible.

But, if he were being honest with himself, he would also admit that there was another reason he didn't want to bring Paris. After he left the mayor's house, he was going to go to the sheriff's station. Sheriff Dodd would probably readily provide information on the days that the girls went missing. He would enjoy the attention, but having Paris there might complicate things.

She wanted to investigate. He knew that, and he was happy to let her help behind closed doors, but the more she tried to investigate in public, the more dust she would stir up, and Sheriff Dodd would be difficult.

Dust like that always caused trouble.

Unlike Helena, Annie and Duke lived in the middle of town. They thrived on the action and had their hands in everything. Natural, Annie would say, because Duke was the mayor, and the mayor needed to know his town. Of course, Annie and Duke were busybodies long before Duke was mayor. In fact, Finn was surprised at how long it took Duke to run for the position.

Duke would be in the office, but Annie had texted him last night to assure him that she would be home. After he knocked and she opened the door, he could smell bacon wafting from the kitchen.

His stomach growled, and Annie smiled. "Right on time. Come on in. I hope you're hungry. I always make too much."

"I think I could find room." Stepping inside, he couldn't help but grin. It was like stepping back in time. He'd spend his fair share of time at Annie and Duke's house as a kid. Annie always made the best cookies, a fact he'd never told Helena for fear of retribution, and it was like nothing had changed. Same faded yellow floral wallpaper in the kitchen and chipped oak cabinets. It's the same cream-colored refrigerator and the small, small, round kitchen table with wooden chairs.

He stared at those chairs. "Annie. You changed the chair cushions. I'm disappointed in you."

With a chuckle, she carried two plates to the table. "I spilled wine on one of the chairs a few years ago, and we couldn't get the stain out. Not even with a little twitch of my nose and eye of newt, so I figured it was the universe telling me it was a time to make a change."

"You didn't really use the eye of a newt, did you?"

"If you mean mustard seed, then yes. If you mean an actual poor newt, then no. Of course not. Have a seat and try out my fancy new pink chair cushions."

Gingerly, Finn sat down. He was a little worried that the chair might break under his weight. "Very comfortable. And thanks for the breakfast, but you could have answered my questions over text."

"You young generation and your phones. I like real conversation, plus it's good to see you, Finn. I know things have been hard with Helena's death, and Paris is back, and I heard what Helena did with the manor. Are you going to buy her half?"

"We haven't really talked about. It's not a priority for either one of us."

"Of course. I'm so sorry. Still, it's good to see the two of you together. I know Helena always that the two of you would..." she blushed. "Never mind. I shouldn't speak on that."

"Speak on what?"

"You know. She thought you two might...reconnect one day." Annie gave him a knowing look. "Maybe that's why she did what she did."

Finn stiffened and leveled Annie a look. "Paris's destiny was not to be with me. Helena made that loud and clear. Not that it's what I'm here to talk about."

"Is it the opening of the ley lines? Heavens, but the town is just dripping in magic. I feel positively drunk on it! What do you think could have caused such a thing? It hasn't acted like that in decades!"

She giggled, and Finn couldn't help but smile. The magic had done Annie good. Her hair was a little shinier, and her eyes brighter. Had they all realized that they'd been living in muted magic? Was it something that Helena had done?

"No, that's not what I'm here to discuss either. Annie, do you know where Helena's grimoire is?"

"Her grimoire? No, of course not. We both know how she guarded it, not that you can blame her. We all guard our books. Heavens, is it missing?"

"I wouldn't say missing," Finn said carefully. The last thing he wanted was for Annie to start spreading rumors that someone had stolen it. "I think Helena might have hidden it. Or even the house.."

She narrowed her eyes. "Oh, that damn manor. Always playing tricks. I don't know why Helena would have spelled her own house, but it is a nightmare. I'm sure it's hiding Helena's book."

Finn didn't think he'd ever heard Annie cuss before. He tried to bite back a laugh. "It does have a little bit of an attitude and some very strong opinions. You didn't see where she put it at the last meeting?"

"Meeting? Coven meeting? Oh, Finn, honey, we haven't had a coven meeting at Helena's house in ages. We've been meeting at Marigold's for...oh, I don't know, five or six years."

"Marigold?" That was Helena's next-door neighbor, but they weren't exactly close. "But Helena is the coven leader."

Annie pursed her lips together and put down her fork. "Helena isn't the coven leader. We didn't move our meeting place because we were tired of the manor. We did it because Helena withdrew from the coven. She didn't give a reason. She just called me one day and said she was done. The coven voted on Marigold to take her place. I hate to speak ill of the dead, especially of Helena, because I did love her so, but for that, I've always hated her a little. She didn't just abandon me. She abandoned Silver Mist."

Shocked, Finn stared at her. "But the ley line..."

"Oh, she still managed it, as far as I could tell, but the less active she was, I think, the less active it was. Did you open it, Finn? Are you the new guardian?"

"No. I'm sorry, Annie. I know that's probably weighing on your mind."

"We had an emergency meeting the night Helena died. We all felt it. Not just her spirit being gone but the ley line being in mourning. When it opened, I just assumed it had chosen a new guardian. As far as I know, it's not someone in the coven. I assume it was her direct descendent. Are you sure?"

"If it is me, you'll be first to know. Well, I'll be the first to know, so you'll be the second to know," he promised.

Annie smiled indulgently. "Now then, let me tell you all the gossip you've missed."

CHAPTER 13
FINN

I t was two hours before Finn could leave. Luckily, the sheriff's station was only a few blocks away. After he parked, he checked his phone, hoping there might be a text from Paris.

There wasn't one.

Not that he should expect a text. They weren't dating. They were just friends who lived together. Maybe she was sleeping in late. Maybe she was busy taking inventory in the house.

Maybe she was applying for a loan so she could buy out his half of the house.

At the last thought, Finn grimaced. He hadn't considered whether Paris could buy him out. He wasn't at the point where he wanted to think about giving up Helena's manor.

Or Paris.

Pocketing his phone, he strolled to the station and opened the door. A familiar face was behind the desk, but Finn couldn't place him. He looked to be close to Finn's age, maybe a few years older, with plenty of salt in his dark hair.

"Hello, deputy? I was hoping I could speak to Sheriff Dobbs. Is he in?"

The deputy looked up at Finn. His eyes were suspiciously glassy. "I am a deputy. You were hoping to speak to Sheriff Dobbs," he said in a monotone voice.

"Yes," Finn said slowly. Was the man high? He glanced at the name tags. "Deputy Wellam?"

"I am Deputy Wellam. Deputy Dash Wellam."

"Okay. I'm Finn. Is Sheriff Dobbs in the office?"

"You are Finn. Sheriff Dobbs is my boss. He is the sheriff."

The man swayed a little, and Finn narrowed his eyes. That wasn't drugs. That was something else entirely. Cautiously, Finn reached out and touched the man's shoulder. He poked just a little, and Dash swayed back and then forward like he was a weeble-wobble toy. They don't fall down.

Spell. He was definitely under a spell.

"Thank you for letting me go back to the office," Finn said carefully as he walked back to the door and flipped the deadbolt to lock them in. He didn't want anyone else walking in until he could figure out what was going on. Then, he stepped around the counter. People under spells could still retain memory, so he wanted to be cautious. Hopefully, when the spell wore off or was reversed, Dash would be none-the-wiser.

"I'm letting you back in the office," Dash said. He didn't move as Finn left him.

There were two deputies at desks in the back room. They were staring at their computers, just as glassy-eyed. No one even acknowledged him.

The door to Dobbs' office was open, and the sheriff was inside, a blank look on his face. He stared at the window.

Finn didn't say a word as he slipped by. Now that he was closer to the back, he heard movement in the records room.

Unsure of what he would find, he stepped cautiously inside. A slender figure in a black hoodie, black jeans, and a black stocking cap was rifling through one of the drawers.

"Paris," he hissed, recognizing the blonde hair spilling out and the curve of her body. "What are you doing?"

With a loud shriek, she whirled around. Contents of a folder went flying to the floor, and she stared at him with the guiltiest look on her face. "Finn. Hi. Fancy meeting you here. Did the sheriff call you in, too?"

Leaning against the wall, he crossed his arms. "Sheriff Dobbs called you in for questioning?"

Turning away, she muttered something under her breath as she started to pick up the contents that had fallen. When she turned back, she flashed all her teeth in a wide smile. "So what are you doing here?"

"What did you do to the people in the office?"

"I...um...well, when I walked in, they were already like that."

"Uh-huh." She couldn't lie. She was terrible at it. "So you cast the spell before you even walked in. Have you lost your mind? You're not practiced in magic, and you're spelling people?"

All pretenses dropped, and she glared at him. "What was I supposed to do? It wasn't like you were interested in helping me!"

"I left you a note that said I would come back this afternoon, and we'd work on your magic."

"Well, I didn't want to wait that long. I would say I did an excellent job casting the spell."

"Uh-huh. And what if someone else had walked into the office? You remember what it's like in this town, right Paris?

Mrs. Flannigan is probably still in here three times a week trying to get her neighbor arrested because his tree blocks the sun to her tulip bed."

She grimaced. "Right. Next time, I'll lock the door."

"Uh-huh. And what about the cameras? They're all over this place, not to mention that some spells don't wipe memories. This is a sheriff's station. If they think something is weird, they might investigate. They know all about what's really happening in this town. They're gonna know it's magic. And why are you in all black? It's not the middle of the night."

"Fine. I messed up, okay? The spell was supposed to let me in unnoticed. I thought it would make me invisible or something, but when I walked in, it was like everyone in the office had smoked a few joints with some hallucinogenic mushrooms. Dash thought I was his high-school girlfriend. He asked me if I wanted to make out under the bleachers."

"Did he now?" Finn growled.

"Stop it," she swatted his chest. "All I wanted was the file from when I went missing, but it's not here."

"Probably because it's in Sheriff Dobbs' office. He's probably had it on hand since the moment you returned. Put that back, and come with me."

Hurriedly, she tossed the folder back into the cabinet and closed the file. "Why does this room even exist? Shouldn't there be digital copies?"

"Yes, but they'd want hard copies in case the computer went down." He grabbed her hand and pulled her toward Dobbs' office.

The sheriff blinked at her. "Susan? Susan, what are you doing here, honey? You should be at school."

"Nope." Finn shook his head and pulled Paris back out

of the office. Apparently, the spell had backfired so that the only person they wanted to talk to was Paris. They just didn't know it was her. "Stay here. Don't move."

Paris nodded, and Finn went back into the office. The sheriff had already returned to his seat. "Sheriff, I'm just going to borrow your finger real quick," he said casually as he pressed the sheriff's finger to the ID on his keyboard. From there, he searched the computer for the camera files for the last hour. He permanently deleted them and then disabled the camera and hoped nothing horrible happened between now and when Dobbs realized the system was down.

Leaving the office, he grabbed Paris's hand and started to tug her to the front but stopped short and turned around. "Are you wearing anything under that shirt?"

Immediately, her cheeks reddened. "Excuse me?"

"Can you take the highly suspicious black hoodie that you're wearing in seventy-degree weather off?"

"Oh. Yes." She took off the black hat and the hoodie. Running her fingers through her blonde hair, she smiled. "Better?"

"Where did you even get a ski cap?"

"Um...well, I was muttering to myself about needing one, and then it was on my bed."

"I'm going to burn the manor to the ground," Finn grumbled. He took her clothes and tugged her outside. "Stay here."

Thankfully, no one was outside. He checked the pockets of her hoodie, pulled out the pieces of paper he found, and dumped the items in a can. "Hey, that hoodie was mine!"

"I'll buy you a new one."

"It belonged to...a friend."

An ex-boyfriend? Now, Finn really didn't feel bad about throwing it away. "Tell me the spell you cast."

"There are spell bags on all four corners of the building. Anyone inside is supposed to just let me in."

That was easy enough. Finn ordered her again not to move and jogged around the building, gathering the bags. In the back and out of sight, he opened them up. A black stone was nestled in some herbs in each bag. It was easy enough to disarm. Collecting the stones, he pocketed them and whispered to the herbs, lulling the magic back to sleep.

Thankfully, Paris hadn't moved. He went to shove the spell back in his pocket, but they were full. Taking out the papers, he put them between his teeth while he pocketed the bags and hurried back to Paris.

"Hey, those are mine!" Paris hissed and grabbed them. Folding them up, she shoved them in her back pocket and avoided his gaze.

He'd find out what those were after he got her away from the sheriff's station.

"All right. Time to see what kind of damage you did." Finn opened the door back to the station and jerked his head. She shot him a look and strolled inside.

"Mrs Hollyman! Hi, good to see you again!"

"Dash, I told you to call me Paris. And for the record, it's Ms. Never been married."

Great, now she was flirting with him? At least he wasn't in a stupor anymore and didn't seem to have any lingering effects from the spell.

"How can I help you?"

"We were hoping to see Sheriff Dobbs. Is he in?" Finn interrupted.

"Sure. He's in his office. Let me just see if he's busy."

Turning his back on them, he picked up the phone. A minute later, he hung up. "He can see you. Follow me."

Dash walked them to the office, and Dobbs was standing. He cleared his throat and glanced around like he was missing something. "Finn. Paris. What can I do for you? Haven't found any other dead bodies, have you?"

"Cute," Paris said dryly.

Finn put a hand to her back, hoping she might keep her temper in check. "Sorry to bother you, Sheriff Dobbs, but we were hoping for a favor. Being back in town has been causing Paris some nightmares. I know what the town thinks, but I think something did happen to her while she was here. Maybe they just got lost. Who knows, but do you think we can take a look at the investigation file? I'm hoping maybe it might put her nightmares to rest."

"I pulled it out the other day, just out of curiosity. Too thin, if you ask me," he said as he opened the drawer. "I'll make a copy of it. Maybe those nightmares are born of guilt."

"If you really thought that, you wouldn't be giving us a copy, now would you?" Paris said coolly.

Dobbs stopped, sighed, and left with the file. A few minutes later, he returned. "This triggers anything that you think might be helpful; you let me know."

Huh. Was the sheriff having second thoughts about what happened? Or maybe just how he'd treated three teenage girls when his office and the FBI came up empty?

"Have you made any leeway with Darren's murder?" Finn asked quietly. "Frankly, I think that is where her nightmares are coming from."

He suspected Dobbs wouldn't give up information on an active case, so he wasn't surprised when the sheriff gave him a cold smile. "I'm not at liberty to discuss the details of an ongoing case. You know how it is."

Finn held his gaze and nodded. "Thank you for your help today."

"Whatever." He dismissed them with a wave of his hand.

When they got outside, Paris held out her hand for the folder, but Finn held it just out of reach. "What's on the papers you're hiding from me?"

"We're not kids anymore, Finn. You can't just hold something over my head and taunt me."

"Couldn't do that anyway. If I remember correctly, that's how I got punched in the gut."

A ghost of a smile played on her face. "I'm happy to help clear up that memory for you."

"Paris."

"Fine." With a huff, she reached into her pocket and pulled out the papers. "They're just other spells I thought I could use. There are some people I want to talk to, and I want the truth."

Quickly, Finn grabbed the spells and relinquished the folder. Sifting through the hastily written instructions, he shook his head in disbelief. "Time to get you home before you make the whole town lose their minds."

"Nobody lost their minds."

"No? Just me then."

CHAPTER 14
PARIS

It danced gently, almost like it was teasing her. Paris narrowed her eyes, focusing on the flame. The exercise had been simple. Create the flame with her magic, but that had gone poorly. Not in the way she thought it might go. She'd lit candles. Easily. Every single candle in the house had come alive, even the one in her bathroom upstairs, but not this one. Oh no. It had taunted her with its darkness. Paris swore Finn was somehow playing tricks on her.

Once Finn had doused the other flames, he'd lit this one with a match and told her to try and put the flame out.

Frustration built inside her. She could feel the magic. When she'd made the spell bags for the sheriff station, she'd never felt so powerful in her life. Now, trying to focus on one thing, she thought she might combust, but for the life of her, she couldn't channel her magic to do what it was supposed to do.

"Forget the candle. Close your eyes. Empty out your mind of everything," Finn said soothingly. "Focus on your breath. Inhale, two, three, four. Exhale, two, three, four.

Inhale, two, three, four. Exhale, two, three, four. Very good.

"Now focus on energy. Feel the chill of your breath going in and the heat going out. That's energy. Feel your body respond to your breath. Rise of your chest. Subtle movements of your shoulders. It's automatic. It's what you've done all your life. Focus on what you feel around you. The slight movement of the air. The way the hairs on your arm stand up. Inhale, two, three, four. Exhale, two, three, four. Listen to your intuition. You know it's magic. It's the magic of this house. The energy that's built up from years of witchcraft. The house is feeding you. The magic in me. You can sense it. You didn't know it then, but it was also automatic. It's always been there. Only now you can access it.

"Just as the magic inside of you has always been there. Inhale, two, three, four. Exhale, two, three, four. You can feel it inside you. Building, just like your emotions. Your needs. Your desires. This isn't just mental, though. It's physical. You can control it. Manipulate it. Focus on what you want that candle to do. You want to put the flame out. Picture it in your mind. The flame winking out of existence. You can do that."

The air moved around her, and she could feel the magic of the house. It was caressing her, making every part of her body feel electric. She focused on the candle. All she had to do was distinguish the candle. Just a little bit of magic, create a void of no oxygen just around the flame, and zip, it would be gone.

"That's it. Focus. When you're ready, open your eyes," he settled his hands on her waist, his breath warm in her ear, "and focus on that flame —oh, no."

He broke off with a curse, and Paris opened her eyes just

in time to see the flame of the candle shoot toward the ceiling. Her heart hammered at the feeling of Finn's hands on her, the heat of him standing that close.

Suddenly, all the candles were lit again, but their flames were just as erratic as her thoughts.

Finn held out his hand, and the candles extinguished. "All right, I think that might be enough for today."

Thunder boomed overhead, and Paris glanced out the window. It was still bright and sunny outside. "Are there supposed to be storms today?"

"No."

The wind whipped at her hair, and she looked up at the ceiling in horror. Was she causing the thunderstorm? In the freaking living room? "Finn?"

"Don't panic. You are in control." He took her hands and gave her a soft smile. "Is the thunderstorm because you're frustrated? Scared? Angry?"

"I like the thunderstorms," she admitted. "I like the chaos. The energy. The...um...passion."

Her cheeks reddened, and Finn cleared his throat. "You're feeling chaotic. That's normal." Thunder boomed again. "But you don't need to manifest the chaos to embrace it, Paris. Focus on your magic. Give it a single command. Any command."

Easier said than done. The magic hadn't done anything that she'd asked it today.

His fingers intertwined with her, and she focused on that. The warmth and comfort that she drew from his touch. The confidence that he had in her. Her magic flowed through her, calmer. Something that she could control.

The image of Helena staring up at the full moon popped into her head. The image of Finn, as a teenager, grinning down at her. Those were in the past, though. They were things she could control. They made her smile, but they weren't what kept her here.

Instead, she stared into Finn's eyes. He wasn't a teenager anymore. Their relationship had changed and shifted with time, and for many years, it was non-existent, but he was here now. Helping her. Teaching her.

He was calm. Grounded. She could feel that flowing through her. A sturdy tree in the storm that she had created.

Turning her head, she focused on the candle. The thunder boomed one last time, and the clouds cleared. "Illuminate," she whispered, and the single candle flared to life.

"Great job. Oh!" He grunted as she threw herself into his arms with a laugh and slid her hands up the back of his head. She felt exhilarated, and an uncontrollable laughter bubbled up inside her.

"I did it! Oh my gosh, I did so much. I feel incredible!"

"It's the magic. It can be intoxicating." He held her gaze for a moment, and heat flared up between them. She thought for sure he might kiss her, but when he put his arms at her waist, it wasn't to draw her in.

Gently, he pushed her away. "It can get a little overwhelming, Paris."

"Or it can give you the courage to do everything you wanted."

It wasn't the magic that made her want to kiss him. It was *him*. Could he really not see that?

Did he just not feel the same way?

The sound of the doorbell interrupted them. With a gasp, she looked up at the ceiling. There wasn't a trace of the storm left. "Do you think anyone else heard the thunder?"

"Only one way to find out." He headed to the front door, and Paris followed closely behind. He glanced through the peephole and frowned. "It's Marigold."

"From next door? Maybe she did hear the thunder." When Finn didn't immediately open the door, Paris studied his face. "Something is wrong."

"I'm not sure. Don't offer up any information about your magic." When she nodded, he opened the door. "Hello, Marigold."

Marigold was a woman in her eighties. Just like Helena remembered, the next-door neighbor still preferred bright and bold makeup and clothes. Tonight, she was swaddled in pink. Her bleached blonde hair was piled up with a bright pink scarf, and pink hoops hung from her ears. She wore a pink dress with darling little yellow flowers. It was all a little over-the-top, but Marigold was always like that. Tonight, there was no hint of the warmth that used to be in her eyes.

She looked tired. And annoyed.

"Finn. Paris. I see the two of you have made yourself at home. So, the rumors are true. Helena left you both the house. Interesting. May I come in?"

Paris didn't like her tone of voice and half-expected Finn to tell her no, but he stepped back and gestured with his hand. Marigold walked inside, and the door slammed forcefully behind her. Marigold jumped and glared at Finn, but Paris knew he hadn't been the one to slam the door.

"Sorry. You know how this manor can be sometimes."

"Hmph. Helena always did like to leak more magic than she could control."

And here, Paris was under the impression that they were supposed to be hiding their powers. "Magic?"

Marigold shot her a withering look. "Don't look so

surprised. I know you're practicing magic. I can sense it, and it's not Finn's kind of magic. Maybe Helena didn't tell you how we do things in Silver Mist, or maybe she did, and like her, you're disregarding the rules, but as a resident witch, it's your responsibility to announce yourself to the coven's head witch."

Paris was even more confused. "Helena is dead, Marigold."

"Me," Marigold snapped. "I'm the head witch. I have been for years."

Finn cleared his throat. "Yes, well, I'd like to point out that simply because Paris inherited a house here doesn't make her a resident. She hasn't moved here permanently."

"Still..."

"Still nothing. If she decides to live here, then she will present herself to the coven. You know she's here. You know she's practicing magic. Is there anything else you want to discuss?"

Marigold was angry, but for the life of her, Paris couldn't figure out why. She didn't know the rules. Was Marigold really going to punish her for that?

"I suppose not," Marigold sniffed and turned to the door. Paris had never loved Marigold, but she didn't want to leave it like this, especially if Marigold was the head of her coven. She quickly intervened.

"Marigold, I am sorry. I don't mean to cause any problems here. When I lived with Helena, I didn't realize I had magic, so Helena never discussed it with me. I've been on my own for a long time. I don't even know what a coven does. If you'll have me, I'd love to come to the next meeting and observe."

"Covens are for members. They are not for people observing," Marigold snapped.

So much for the peace offering.

"Before you go, Marigold, there is something that I wanted to ask you. I also didn't know that you were the head of the coven until I spoke to Annie this morning. Maybe you can help me."

Marigold sighed and turned. "With what?"

"Helena's grimoire is missing. I don't suppose you know where it is."

"Young man, are you suggesting that I stole her grimoire? How dare you!"

Finn cocked his head. "I didn't suggest anything, Marigold. I asked Annie the same question. She assumed maybe I was hoping she'd seen where Helena kept it. You, on the other hand, jumped to theft. Interesting."

"There's nothing interesting about that. I just know what you think, Finn. I've taken nothing from Helena. Nothing from this house!"

The manor began to tremble beneath their feet, and Paris felt an overwhelmingly furious energy rush over her. The anger nearly took her breath away. Marigold gasped and pressed a hand over her heart. "I hate this manor," she snarled. "Get your house under control."

She practically tripped over her own two feet as she raced out and slammed the door behind her. The trembling stopped, and Paris and Finn stared at each other. "If I didn't know better, I'd say that she was hiding something."

Finn nodded. "I couldn't agree more. Manor, I don't suppose you have anything to say about it?"

The house fell silent. So much for a magical witness.

CHAPTER 15
PARIS

Unable to sleep that night, Paris sat up in bed and poured over the copy of the skinny file Sheriff Dobbs had given them.

There was very little in the file that she didn't already know. According to Helena, Ginger's mom, and Sage's dad, the last time they saw them was at dinner on a Thursday night. It wasn't uncommon for them to get together in the evening, especially in the summer. At that age, they'd stay out until midnight or later. Silver Mist Cove was a safe town. Weird, but safe.

Paris didn't remember anything about the day, so she couldn't recall where she and the others had planned to go.

Helena and the parents reported them missing in the morning. A town-wide search began. The next morning, the active sheriff, Sheriff Mills, called the FBI.

Tourists were searched and interviewed. A tip line was set up and immediately dogged with psychics who claimed to know where they were or where their bodies might be found. Every tip was investigated on the off chance that the kidnappers were phoning in.

Paris's parents flew in on that third day. The sheriff had made notes about the tension between them and Helena.

Then, Bobby had called. The teenagers had stumbled out of the woods where he and Susan were camping. Bobby was interviewed and dismissed as a suspect. Paris and her friends were taken to the city hospital to be evaluated.

There was nothing wrong with them. No injuries. Not even mild hydration. It was like they'd been gone for an hour-long stroll. Their clothes weren't even dirty.

Magic, Pairs thought as anger rushed over her. It had to be magic. No way their clothes weren't dirty after three days, even if they were faking it.

Helena had to have known, right? She must have used her magic to find the truth. Somewhere in the house, in Helena's grimoire or in her journals, were her notes about those missing days. Maybe Helena even knew what had happened, but she just never told anyone. Not even Paris.

The argument Paris and Helena had the morning before she left with her parents was forever burned in her memory. Fed up with Helena's blasé attitude about the days Paris was missing, she'd screamed at Helena for not caring. Accused her of siding with the rest of the town and thinking she had made it up. Helena had just looked at her and told her that it was good Paris was leaving. Silver Mist Cove wasn't the right place for her.

She'd known right then that Helena was keeping secrets. She could see it in the way the older woman had shifted her eyes away.

Pairs skimmed the rest of the file, but she already knew the rest. They were tested for drugs. Questioned like suspects. Even poly-graphed. It had been terrifying.

But she wasn't a scared eighteen-year-old anymore,

and she knew the truth about the town. Magic was on her side.

Annie had mentioned that Darren liked to date married women. Maybe his death had nothing to do with her missing time, but someone knew something. Darren was key. Tomorrow, she'd corner one and see what they had to say.

THE NEXT MORNING, she decided to take Finn's lead and slip out before breakfast. She still wasn't sure she could face him after the almost-kiss and the firm rejection. It was fine. Finn didn't feel the same. She was an adult, and she could handle it.

Just not at that very moment.

So she left and gave him a quick text so he'd know where she was. Even that felt a little too intimate, but he'd been leaving her notes, so that was the least she could do.

It was too early to look up the first of her suspects, so she went to the diner first to get some breakfast. After avoiding two offers for a palm reading and one offer to read the freckles on her arm (that was new), she drove to Ginger's old house.

It was just how she remembered it. A blue bungalow-style home with pale yellow trim. The paint was faded, and the weeds had overtaken the gravel driveway. Most of the landscape was bare, but the yard was mowed.

Paris couldn't help but wonder how Ginger felt about it. Her mother always had a beautiful front yard filled with life. Big blooms for the bees and butterflies. Bird feeders and houses.

Whoever did maintain it for renters did the bare minimum. Would Ginger do anything to it before she sold it?

Would she sell?

Knowing that it was early, Paris went up and knocked softly on the door. There was a muffled argument on the other side of the door before it opened, and a teenager looked at her with exasperation.

For a moment, Paris thought she'd done a spell and gone back in time. The girl looked almost exactly like Ginger when she was that age.

Except, instead of Ginger's bright blue eyes, the daughter had dark eyes and slightly darker skin.

She scowled at her. "I swear, if you are here to give me a reading, I'm going to scream so loud."

Paris couldn't help but grin. Clearly, someone wasn't as enchanted with the local residents as others. "Silver Mist Cove is an acquired taste," she chuckled. "You must be Ivy. I'm Paris. I'm a friend of your mother's."

"Huh." Ivy looked her up and down with a critical eye. "Mom. It's for you, just like I said it would be because I don't know anyone in town because you took me away from all my friends."

"I can hear you just fine, Ivy, as can the rest of the street," Ginger sighed as she walked around the corner. "Paris! Oh, did we say we were going to meet up this morning? I must have forgotten."

"We didn't make any plans. I was just planning on doing some...errands today, and I thought you might like to join me." Paris didn't want to come right out and say investigate in front of Ivy.

"Errands? Oh! Errands. Right. Umm...." she looked behind her. "I had some things to do around the house, and there's Ivy."

The teenager snorted. "Mom, please. I'm sixteen. I think I can survive on my own for a couple of hours. I wanted to call some friends. You know, the ones we left when we moved?"

Ginger rolled her eyes. "Yes. You might have mentioned those friends once or twice. Promise that you'll unpack at least one box while I'm gone?"

"Fine. Whatever."

"The kitchen is fully stocked. Please don't leave the house, even for a walk, without texting me first."

"Like I want to go for a walk." Ivy scowled and walked around the corner, muttering something under her breath.

Ginger gave Paris an unapologetic look. "She's still a little unhappy about the move."

"Move, so this is permanent?"

"For now. I have some things to work out. Let me just grab my purse, and then you can tell me about these errands you want to run."

An hour later, it was like no time had passed at all. Any awkwardness from the last two silent decades had evaporated by the time Paris parked. "You were the one who dyed it green! It absolutely was not me," she protested as she turned to Ginger. "You wanted to impress David Cook, and green was his favorite color."

"No," Ginger laughed as she wiped the tears from her eyes. She thought about it for a minute and widened her eyes. "Oh, you're right. It was me!"

"It was, and when we got in trouble for it, it was Sage who decided we could clean it with soap," Paris confirmed. They looked at each other and cracked up again at the memory. The fountain in the middle of the town square had never looked so good. Green suds had gone all the way down Main Street. It was a nightmare.

When they settled, Ginger looked out the window. "The

print shop? Are you planning on putting up some posters with a tip line or something?"

"No. I need to print my invoices for the last few months."

Ginger wrinkled her nose. "I know that voice. We are not here on errands, and you do not need to go to a print shop to print invoices. What's really going on, Paris?"

"Rumors are that Darren liked his women married. Marsha Milton is one of the women he was reportedly seeing. She owns the print shop."

"Oh. Do you think it was a jilted woman or maybe her jilted husband who did Darren in? That means it might not have anything to do with what happened to us."

"True, and after all this time, it probably doesn't have anything to do with us. But he was found in Helena's house, so he was there for something. Once we find who killed him, we'll know why he was there. Hopefully."

"That makes sense. Marsha Milton," Ginger repeated to herself. "I don't recognize the name."

"Me either, which is why we can't just walk in and strike up a conversation for old times sakes. I'm going to go in, request the print job, and while we're there, you're going to ask me questions about Darren. Hopefully, we get a response from her."

"I can certainly ask you some questions. I don't know anything about the man."

"Perfect. It'll feel authentic."

"Do you expect her to come right out and say they were having an affair and that she killed him in a passionate rage?"

No, especially since Finn made it very clear that she was not to cast any more spells to get information. "You and I both know how rumors can be. I'm hoping, from her expression, that we'll be able to see if there's any truth to it. If they are having an affair, I wonder how much she'll open up to us. It's just like you said, and she wasn't here when we were growing up, so she shouldn't recognize us."

"Unless Darren told her about us."

"Exactly."

They walked confidently into the print shop. It was empty, as Paris suspected it might be on a weekday morning, and approached the counter. It was a small shop, and unlikely that Marsha had a lot of employees working for her. Hopefully, she was in.

"Hello," Paris said brightly as she walked up to the counter.

"Just a minute." The muffled answer came from behind the closed door. A minute later, it opened, and an attractive woman in her late forties or early fifties walked out. "My name is Marsha. How can I help you?"

"Those are the words I want to hear. I just came back to town a few days ago, and I just cannot get the printer working at the place I'm staying. I just have a small print job and was hoping you could help me out." Paris put on her customer service face with her best peppy voice. She used it to put her clients at ease. Hopefully, it would do the same for Marsha.

"Printing is what we do! When do you need it by?"

"When I say small, I mean small. It's not even a dozen pages. Is it possible you could do it now?"

Marsha gave her a bright smile. "I think I can do that. Just email it to Printservices at MarshaPrints dot com."

Paris made a show of trying to pull up her email. "I'm so sorry, this might take a minute. My phone is so slow. I really need to switch to a new provider."

"I'm assuming that's why you didn't text me right away

when you found a body in your house," Ginger said quickly. "Because you need a new provider."

Not the smoothest transition, and it was a little too enthusiastic, but it did the trick. "I had to call the police first," Paris said dryly and looked at her phone again. "Okay, here we go."

"Body?" Marsha asked with interest. "You don't mean Darren, do you? You're the one who found him?"

Ginger gasped. "Did you know him? Oh, I'm so sorry. How callous of me, bringing him up like that."

"Oh, no. People have been talking about him since it happened. A lot of people knew Darren. Small town and all. I was sorry to hear about his death. We were...friends, I suppose. He lived in on my street."

"Your neighbor and your friend! Again, I am so sorry. Oh my gosh, Marsha," Ginger whispered theatrically. "Marsha Milton. I didn't make the connection, but you were his girl-friend! I am so sorry."

"Girlfriend," All pretenses of friendliness dropped as Marsha said with narrow eyes. "Where did you hear that from?"

"I don't even remember. Should I not have said anything?"

Fearing Ginger was pushing a little hard, Paris cleared her throat. "Email is sent, I believe! My address is Paris Hollyman at Paris Designs."

Marsha continued to stare at Ginger, waiting for her to answer her question, but Ginger stepped away and pretended to read one of the signs posted on the wall. Finally, Marsha sighed.

"Got it right here." She turned her focus on the computer for a few minutes while she clicked the mouse. The silence built between them, and when she turned, Paris was taken off guard to see that tears had welled up in Marsha's eyes. "I'm happily married, and any rumors that Darren and I were together are false. I would appreciate it if you told other people the same. I'm sure you, of all people, know what it's like to be the victim of a false rumor, don't you, Ms. Hollyman?"

She did recognize them, or at least she recognized the names. That didn't mean anything. She'd heard it from Darren. Most of the town knew who they were.

The words were effective, though, and. Ginger reached across and squeezed her hand. "We do understand, and we promise we'll squash any rumors that we hear. I'm so sorry for the misunderstanding."

"Darren and I were friends. Good friends. When my marriage was rocky, Darren was there for me, but not like that. Never like that. Maybe I let my husband get a little jealous so he would just try harder, but I never crossed a line."

"Marsha, do you have any idea why Darren would have been in Helena's house that night?" Paris murmured.

Marsha opened her mouth, but before she could answer, the bell sounded over the door. "Do you just need one copy?" She asked brightly, clearly more than happy to change the subject

They'd lost her. Paris nodded. "Yes, one copy."

"Excellent. That won't take long at all. Be with you in a minute," Marsha called over Paris's shoulder and disappeared in the back.

Ginger looked over her shoulder and froze. Paris followed suit. A tall and willowy brunette walked toward them. The face was familiar, but Paris couldn't immediately place it.

The look on her face was nothing short of predatory.

113

"Ginger Mayes, back in Silver Mist. Or is it something else? Did you get married, Ginger?" The woman asked in a sweet voice.

"Hello, Dana," Ginger said coolly. "And I did get married, but it's still Ginger Mayes."

"Hmph. Here for Helena's funeral, I suppose."

"Yes, and no. I think I might stick around for a while."

The woman narrowed her eyes until they were just thin slits. "I hope you're not planning on picking up your mother's mantle. The headliner is mine. Mine and my daughters. Has been for years."

"That's sweet, Dana. A mother-daughter act. I did a few shows with my mother, as I'm sure you'll remember. I wonder if my daughter would be interested." The picture of innocence, Ginger turned toward Paris. "What do you think? The Mayes's legacy could continue. My mother would be so pleased."

Instantly, it clicked for Paris. Dana Blanche. She tried so hard to be their friend when she was a teenager, and for a summer, they were open to it. Dana was funny, sweet, and new to the town. There was no reason for them not to be until it became clear that Dana was just using Ginger to get to her mother in an attempt to get in on her act. She was, as Dana had once said, a real psychic, unlike Ginger, who was clearly just performing on stage.

Once they'd spurned her for that, Dana had turned on them. With the residential population being as small as it was, teenagers were either friends or enemies. There was no in-between.

Obviously, Dana still harbored an intense dislike for them. Ginger, who was bar none the nicest person Paris had ever met, wasn't even trying to bridge the gap between them. Clearly, she was still pissed at Dana, and

Paris couldn't blame her. Dana was just being straight-up rude.

"Ginger and Ivy Mayes," Paris said as she swept her hand through the air. "Second and third generation...no, I'm sorry, your grandmother performed as well. Third and fourth-generation psychics. The act that everyone would flock to see. It has a ring to it."

"What are you even doing here," Dana snapped angrily, turning her anger to Paris. "You and Helena didn't even speak for years. Not after that stunt you two and your little friend pulled. This town supported Helena after you left. She withdrew into that manor of hers. I bet you never even wondered what your false cry for help did to her, and now you're here, crying on Finn's shoulder. Yeah, like he won't see right through that."

Paris blinked. That was a lot of accusations in one breath. If she didn't know how quickly the town would latch on to Dana's ideas, she would have laughed. Did she really think, for a moment, that she was just here because of Finn?

Marsha cleared her throat. "Your order is ready."

Paris turned and handed Marsha her debit card. Marsha's eyes darted toward Dana for a moment before they returned to Paris. "Darren is not what you think he is," she said in a low voice. "I hope you'll believe that."

What did she mean by that? Paris wanted to ask for more, but it was clear that Marsha wasn't going to offer any additional information, not with Dana standing there, tapping her toe on the floor.

"Thank you," Paris said with a smile as she took her package. She turned and side-stepped Dana, but Ginger walked right up to her.

"It's dangerous to go spouting theories when you know

nothing about them," Ginger said in a low voice. "I only hope you never know what it feels like to have the town you called home, the neighbors you grew up with, the people you respected and supported turn on you."

Dana inhaled sharply, but Ginger didn't stop. "This is a weird place. Sometimes people get exactly what they deserve."

They exited the shop. Trouble brewed on Ginger's face, but Paris didn't say anything until they were in the car. Ginger had said this was a weird place. Did she know the truth about Silver Mist?

"Are you okay?" Paris asked softly.

"I'm fine, but I think I've done all the sleuthing I've got in me." Ginger shot her a smile as fake as the diamond earrings that had been in Dana's ears. "Do you think you can take me home? I need to check on my daughter."

"Of course. And if you're planning on staying Ginger, don't worry. Nothing is going to happen to Ivy. We'll all make sure of it."

CHAPTER 16

PARIS

Paris dropped Ginger off and headed back to town. While she grabbed a coffee, she looked at the second name on her list. Annabelle Porter. Another name she didn't recognize. She contemplated calling Annie and asking for any details she might have on Annabelle, but she had to be careful. If Annie found out that she was investigating the past, she'd fret. And lecture. And probably cease to provide any information at all.

But Annie didn't have to know that Darren was connected to the past. As long as Paris worded everything right, there wouldn't be any problems.

"Paris!" Annie seemed delighted when she answered the phone. "I was just about to call you. I heard about that nastiness with Marigold."

"Should I apologize to her? I didn't mean to imply that we thought she stole the book." Although Marigold had a jealous streak a mile wide, now she was head of the coven. Maybe she thought there were powerful enough spells in Helena's book that would keep her on top.

"No." Annie's voice dropped all pretense of cheeriness.

"There is no need to apologize to her. Come to dinner tonight. We'll talk about it a little further."

Dinner would give her an excuse to put off facing Finn for a little bit longer. Paris readily agreed before realizing that Annie was about to hang. "One more thing," she said quickly. "I was wondering what you could tell me about Annabelle Porter."

"She's a psychic, my dear, not that helps you at all," Annie chuckled. "She has her own shop, though. It's an impressive feat, considering she only moved here a few years ago. Most new people don't make it long, but she seems to be very popular with the tourists. She is not much of a showman, so she doesn't do anything on stage. Why are you asking about her?"

Paris chose her words carefully. "You'd said that she might have been seeing Darren, along with Marsha. I wanted to try to get to know the man a little better. He did die in the manor, and I feel so uneasy about it."

"Oh, yes. Why didn't I think of that? A violent energy would certainly leave residue in the manor. Knowing that house, I'm surprised it hadn't cleansed itself. Do you want me to come over and do a cleansing for you, dear?"

"No, no. I'm not looking to cleanse the energy just yet. I want to get to know it a little better, and I think I can do that if I get to know Darren a little better. I went to see Marsha today, but unfortunately, Ginger and I ran into an old acquaintance that made the whole visit unpleasant. I'm sure you know Dana Blanche?"

"Insufferable woman, but she does put on a good show," Annie muttered. "I had no idea that the two of you have history."

"It's more Ginger than me."

"Ginger. I'm so pleased that she's back. I do hope that

you, Ginger, and Sage can reconnect while you're here. You three were formidable as friends. I know much time has passed that those kinds of bonds don't just dissolve over time. You'll find your footing. As for Annabelle, you can find her on Divine Street. I think it's called Crystal Bell Readings."

"Thanks, Annie."

They finalized dinner plans, and Paris hung up. After a few minutes of debating, she texted Finn and let him know that she had dinner plans, but she could return to the manor to take Sugar out. He texted back to say that he would walk the dog.

Maybe he also didn't want her to come back.

She told herself that it was fine and headed to her car. She was only gone for about ten minutes, but there were four pamphlets stuck under the windshield. Without reading them, she tossed them in the car and headed to Divine Street.

When she was growing up, the main square was prime real estate for occult shops, but according to the information she'd pulled off the town website the other day, Divine Street was the new hot spot for psychic readings. When she parked on the street and got out, she couldn't help but marvel at how it had changed. Divine Street used to be a small side street that led to a neighborhood. Now, it was a sprawling commerce center.

Crystal Bell Readings was right in the center. Annabelle was lucky indeed to have gotten such a good spot.

The bell over the door rang as Paris walked in, and immediately, the little hairs on her skin stood up. There was a strange energy about this place. One she hadn't felt anywhere else.

"Hello! Welcome to Crystal Bell Readings," a deep voice

said, and a young man in his late twenties walked around the counter. "We sell specialty divination items, prophetic teas, books, candles, and more. And we offer readings by appointment."

He stopped a few feet from Paris, and his warm smile faded just a little as he cocked his head. "Although I get the sense that you aren't here for any of those things."

A slight tingle went down Paris's spine, and she got the oddest sense that the man was actually looking at her. Seeing her. It made her feel a little vulnerable.

Paris cleared her throat, and the man blinked and blushed. "I'm sorry. I hope I didn't make you uncomfortable. I haven't seen anyone with your aura before. It's fascinating."

"My aura?"

"That's my specialty. I'm an aura reader. I'd love to read you more fully if you're interested."

The intensity of his gaze was gone, and that customer service voice was back. Paris couldn't help but chuckle. "I bet you say that to all the women who come in here. I'm actually looking for the store owner. Annabelle Porter."

"She's my mother." His voice took on a protective edge.

"That explains your gift. I heard she's the best, and I'd like to make an appointment with her." It wasn't exactly a lie, and clearly, she needed to get on his good side.

Immediately, the smile was back, and Paris felt a little guilty about the minor deception. Still, a private reading seemed the fastest way to talk to Annabelle privately. After what happened with Marsha this morning, privacy seemed to be key with these kinds of conversations.

"Let me see what she has available." He walked back behind the counter and looked over the computer. "There's an opening tomorrow morning. Ten am."

"That would be perfect."

"And your name?"

"Sarah," Paris lied. "Sarah Brown." There was no need to give out her real name since, apparently, after all this time, it was still so well known.

"All right, Ms. Brown, we'll see you tomorrow at ten. Care to take a look at our preparation teas? It's not a requirement, but they help open the senses for the reading. Only five dollars, and it makes a dozen cups."

Paris bought the tea and a few trinkets she found interesting. She wouldn't brew the tea, but it would be interesting to ask Finn if he thought it was genuine or not.

Or, she could ask Annie. The woman was in Helena's coven. Annie would be an excellent source of magical information. Maybe even a mentor.

It was a strange new chapter in her life. Who would have guessed that Paris would be learning a whole new part of herself at this age?

A part of her that she always felt was missing, even if she didn't know why.

It was easy to lose herself in the town and exercise her new intuition and magical sight. Finn had warned her that if she wasn't careful, she'd over-extend herself, and when her phone vibrated to let her know it was time for dinner, she was drained.

Really drained.

Dragging herself to the car, she managed to get in and close her eyes. She needed to call Annie and tell her that she wasn't going to be able to make it, but she wasn't sure that she would be able to drive herself home.

Paris.

At first, she wasn't even certain she heard anything. She glanced around the car, but she was empty.

Paris.

Starkly, she realized that she wasn't hearing the whisper with her ears. It was in her mind.

"Helena?" She whispered. "Helena, are you in my head? I'm not sure that I'm comfortable with that."

Her windshield clouded from grey to black. Little flecks of silver and blues began to swirl, and Paris stared, mesmerized.

Focus on the darkness, Paris. Let it draw you in. Lose yourself in it.

It wasn't Helena. At least, it was, but not a ghost of her. It was a memory.

She'd been a child only a few days after meeting Helena for the first time. Then, Helena hadn't felt like an aunt or a mentor. She'd just been a strange old woman with a house that smelled weird.

The day had been exhausting. She'd raced around the house all day, exploring whatever nook and cranny she could find. Stuffing herself with the cookies that Helena was feeding her.

Then, she blinked and suddenly felt weak. Drained.

A lot like how she felt now.

Helena had found her curled up in the corner and shaking. Paris had been scared, but Helena had guided her to her bedroom and sat her down in the middle of the bed. She'd placed a medium-sized black mirror in front of her and told her to watch it carefully. In her exhausted state, it was easy to stare at the inky darkness.

She had no idea how much time had passed. She'd assumed she'd fallen asleep, and when she blinked, she was staring at a normal mirror. Helena was in the corner, humming to herself and knitting. Paris had felt fine, and Helena had taken her into town for ice cream.

Staring at the windshield now was like staring in that mirror, but she was no longer in the dark about her abilities. This wasn't a nap or meditation. This was magic.

How was she doing it?

See the pretty colors, Paris? Imagine them reaching out to you, wrapping around your body, dancing on your skin. Don't be scared. They aren't hurting you. They like you, don't they?

They did like her. As the lights filled her car, Paris smiled giddily. It was the same feeling she'd had last night. Drunk on magic.

She had no idea what it was, but instantly, she started to feel better. The colors dissolved. The darkness receded, and she was staring at the sunny street once again.

"Helena, once I figure out what happened to me, you're next," Paris muttered to herself. "Just because you're dead doesn't mean I won't find all your secrets."

But that was later. Now, she had a quiet dinner to enjoy with Annie.

THERE WERE a dozen women bustling around the kitchen. Four pots were bubbling on the stove, and the counters were filled with vegetables and herbs. Five women were chopping. One was standing on the kitchen table, hanging greenery bundles on the chandelier. And another was dancing round the kitchen, humming loudly, and waving a lit candle in the air.

No one had heard her knock at the door, so Paris had let herself in. No one even noticed, and Annie was nowhere to be found.

This was hardly the low-key dinner she'd been looking forward to. If she slipped out now, no one would even know.

Indecision warred inside her. If Annie had invited these women here, she had a good reason that she wanted Paris to meet them.

Paris stood too long, trying to decide what to do when the humming stopped. The chopping stopped.

Everyone stared at her.

Hesitantly, she lifted her hand. "Hi. I'm sorry to interrupt. Is Annie here?"

"You're Paris! Oh my goodness, I would recognize you anywhere! You look just like your mother!"

"I...what? Oh!"" Paris grunted as a woman raced toward her and enveloped her in a hug. "You knew my mother?"

"Oh, yes. I am so happy that you've finally embraced your magic. There is so much we can tell you. Things we can teach you!"

Paris's gaze moved over the women, and slowly, some of their faces grew familiar. "You're Helena's coven," she said softly. "I remember seeing some of you at the house, whispering your secrets together."

"Secrets we can now share with you. Come inside. Please. Annie, the guest of honor, has arrived!"

Annie popped into the kitchen, and for the next ten minutes, Paris was passed around from person to person. Names and faces blurred together, but Paris couldn't believe the excited energy in the air. It started to feel overwhelming.

"All right," Annie said loudly. "Let's sit down for dinner and give Paris some room to breathe. Ladies, can you help me set the table and bring the food out."

They immediately turned and flurried about the kitchen and out. Annie turned to Paris and grabbed her hands. "I should have asked if this was okay, but this is a classic case of begging for forgiveness rather than asking for permission. I hope you don't mind, but I wanted you to see that you are not alone in this new chapter of your life. There are so many people waiting to support you."

"That's very sweet." Paris gave her a reassuring smile. "And you are forgiven."

"Good. I wanted to warn you ahead of time that their excitement that you've come into your magic isn't simply because they want to teach you. Helena spoke of you often during coven meetings. She has always set you up as an heir of some sort. They aren't happy with Marigold at the head of the coven. They haven't been in a long time. I've been talking them down, but they're not listening to me. Tonight, they're going to ask you to take over. I just wanted to prepare you."

"Take over? The coven? Annie, are you serious? I nearly drained myself today just walking around and using the magic to feel and see the town for what it was. I can't lead anyone."

"It's not about how much you know, Paris. That will come. For now, it's about helping to stabilize their magic. That is all about raw power. Some are here to see if you have that. I have never doubted Helena. I know you do. You don't have to make a decision now. Some of them just want to know if you plan on leaving right after the funeral. Just be open to them. Listen to them. Get to know them."

"Is that all?" Paris laughed nervously. "I just discovered I have magic less than a week ago. How bad can Marigold be?"

"Bad."

"Surely you or someone else here can be the head of the coven. You don't need to rely on me."

"We all have a natural inclination to magic, of course. Some of our sisters are more powerful than others. When we perform more powerful spells, the head of the coven is there for balance. She has to be powerful enough to absorb any erratic magic and provide magic if enough isn't there. Marigold struggles."

"So would I."

"You just have to believe in yourself, Paris. That's part of what tonight is about. Surrounding yourself with people who will help you see yourself for the witch that you are." Annie turned and gestured to the door. "Shall we?"

CHAPTER 17
FINN

The forest always came alive at night. During the day, it saw people. Hikers, outside yoga and meditation enthusiasts, and people just looking to get away. They walked through the forest and reveled in the life under the sun. There was plenty of it then, too. Birds flocking and singing. Deer, coyotes, and foxes skipping through the brush. Reptiles slithering and scampering here and there.

So much life during the day, but it was a different atmosphere at night. Sure, those elements were still there, but they were wilder and more raw. The night owls literally owned the skies, and everything felt just a little more feral under the moon.

The magic acted the very same.

Finn was better at wielding his magic at night. His magical senses were sharper, stronger then. It used to drive his mother and Helena crazy because nobody else in the family had those "issues," as they liked to call it. Privately, Finn didn't think of them as issues. He liked the night, and he knew that magic was never going to be the primary force in his life as it had been for Helena.

Tonight especially, he was thankful that his magic was more potent at night. This was not a spell that he could perform during the day. He wasn't even sure it would work tonight, but he had to try.

In digging through Darren's public files, he discovered something very interesting.

At the tender age of twenty-two, Darren moved to Silver Mist. He had no family in town and didn't move for a job. Nobody moved to Silver Mist for a job unless they were hoping to get their big break on the psychic circuit, except that Darren never claimed to be psychic. He got a job as a barista and lived in one of the apartments on the outskirts of town. He was quiet and kept to himself.

And it was two months before Paris, Ginger, and Sage were kidnapped.

Paris believed that Darren was one of her kidnappers. The timing was right, but there wasn't any apparent motive.

Then, six months after Paris had fled town, Darren had been caught breaking into a car. Helena's car.

It was not a coincidence, but for some reason, the incident stayed quiet. Helena had never said anything to Finn, and neither had anyone else. It was still on his record, but if anyone in town had known, the label of thief would have stayed with him.

Too many secrets. Too many things that didn't add up.

Tonight, Finn wanted to see if there was anything he could pick up from the earth from the time the women had gone missing. Time eroded away evidence. Nature washed it away, baked it, froze it, and ate it. There was no point in searching for anything physical, especially, but emotions were another thing entirely.

Emotions lingered for decades. Centuries. Strong emotions could be found in antique furniture, clothes, and jewelry. Anything that wasn't cleansed properly held onto emotional residue.

The same was true for magical residue, and Finn was looking for both. He started on the edge of the property, where the women stumbled out of the forest. Sitting cross-legged on the forest bed, he closed his eyes and placed his hands on the leaves. In one pocket, he had an amplifier crystal, one he'd been charging for an entire lunar cycle, and herbs in his pocket to increase his focus.

"*Speak to me,*" Finn forced his magic into the earth, breathing into it, waking it up. "*Release what does not belong to you.*"

Closing his eyes, he felt a wash of emotion. Childish wonder and glee. Children shed emotion with every step that they take. They didn't know how to filter it or contain it. Finn couldn't help but smile as he brushed it aside and pushed his magic deeper into the woods.

Grief. Someone stood on this spot and wept. That was also something he expected to find. Nature tended to strip away societal fears. Here, no one was watching. No one was judging. It was a safe place to release any emotions that had been bottled up. Grief was one of those emotions that was on every branch of the forest. Finn brushed it aside and surged his magic deeper.

Love and lust. Fear. Confusion. Finn continued to sort, but he knew that if he didn't find what he was looking for soon, he'd burn out, and this wasn't something he could stop and start again.

He pushed deeper. Asked for more.

Just before he tapped out, he requested something different. Something he wasn't sure he could do.

"Speak to me. Release what disturbs you."

Could nature be disturbed? It couldn't sift through emotion like he could. It wouldn't know the difference between grief and fear, but it might feel something that disturbed the balance of nature.

Like three women, drenched in the magic of someone else, panicked for their lives.

Then, he felt it. Fear. Confusion. Anxiety. All bundled up, so strong that it nearly flattened Finn to the ground.

Paris. Oh, he could feel her. It wasn't that her emotions were stronger than Sage's or Gingers, but he knew her. He recognized her.

If he didn't pull himself together, he'd lose the magic or lose himself to the magic. Gritting his teeth, he pushed his magic back into the earth. *"Show me,"* he thundered. *"Show me the path of the disturbance. Light the way."*

It was dim, but when Finn looked up, he saw the gold glittery path leading into the forest. Erratic, but it was something Finn could follow.

Knowing it wouldn't last long, Finn jumped to his feet and raced through the path. Branches gave way, roots sank into the earth, and the path was as easy to navigate as a sidewalk in a neighborhood.

The forest fed him as he ran, feeding its magic to him as his continued to seep out. Soon, he wasn't sure of the difference between his magic and the magic of the woods, but his path continued to glow, and he continued to run.

Whispers rose from the ground. Their whimpers of confusion and cries of anxiety. Finn breathed through it, focused on himself to keep it from consuming him.

Then, abruptly, the path stopped.

Finn looked over his shoulder to make sure the spell was still working. Behind him, golden sparks danced through the air, but in front of him, nothing.

"No." Running his hand through his hair, he looked around. "No."

This was not where the girls had been held for three days. It wasn't possible. They were in the middle of the forest. There was no shelter. There wasn't even a place to erect a temporary shelter.

Twenty-five years ago, the landscape would have looked different, but these were old trees. Ancient trees. They would still have been big and crowded together. Enough for two people to stand but not enough space for a tent or a trailer.

Kneeling down, he places his hands on the ground again. *"Speak to me,"* he commanded. *"Show me the magic here."*

The result was powerful. An immense amount of magic erupted from the earth. Enough residue to have powered several spells all on its own.

Something big happened here. Something powerful here. Paris didn't have any magic then. Ginger and Sage weren't magical. This was someone else's magic.

Darren? If he was a witch, no one in town seemed to know about it.

"Hello? Are you okay?"

Finn ripped his hand away from the ground and looked up as a man emerged from the darkness. "Finn. Are you all right?"

It took a moment to place the voice and the face. Finn rose and brushed off his pants. "Zane. Sorry. I tripped."

"Sure. Went for a run. Tripped over a root. It happens."

Zane walked closer and sniffed. "I'll just ignore the fact that you're dripping in magic."

"Hey, I'm an old man now. Sometimes it takes a little magic to keep me going."

Zane smiled and stretched out his hand. "It's good to see you, Finn. I was sorry to hear about your aunt."

Returning the smile, Finn accepted the hand. He and Zane went to high school together. As hot-headed teenagers, they were more competitive rather than friendly.

Luckily, that competitive streak didn't continue in adulthood, especially since Finn and Zane both moved away.

"Thank you. Are you here for her funeral?"

"No, I moved back two years ago."

"You did? Really?" Shaking his head, Finn held up his hand. "Sorry. That's your business. I shouldn't pry."

Zane was a werewolf. There's much of a werewolf population in Silver Mist. They were sensitive to magic, and the magic here could be overwhelming. Zane was raised by a single mother, a human single mother who didn't know anything about werewolves. She was a psychic. A real psychic, but one who didn't show well. She made her living cold-reading for those on the stage.

"It's all right. Let's just say that my mother was right. I wasn't one who belonged in a pack. You want company on your jog back?"

"Actually, I think I'm going to walk. What exactly are you doing in the forest tonight?"

"I was going for a run, too."

Considering that they were both in jeans, it was easy to see that they were both lying to each other. They fell into step quietly next to each other.

"You know, my return to the town wasn't nearly as interesting as yours. Sharing the house with an old girl-friend. Dead body. All I got was a flux of my mother's old clients asking if she was willing to come out of retirement. I had to tell them that my mother's very happy in Florida, and I have no desire to make other people rich."

"I don't know what to tell you, Zane. I guess I was just more well-liked than you. Red carpet treatment." He chuckled dryly. "And Paris is not an old girlfriend."

"You just wanted her to be."

"You're still annoying."

"You find me annoying? And here I thought we were going to be such good friends." Zane stopped suddenly, grabbed Finn's arms, and sniffed.

Finn immediately stilled. When Zane backed up, Finn followed suit. His magic might have been more powerful at night, but Zane's senses were better at night, and he clearly smelled someone coming.

It was a popular forest. No reason to hide from someone walking at night, but Zane clearly wanted to keep a low profile.

They crouched behind some bushes, and sure enough, a slender woman came into view. Silvery blonde hair gleamed in the moonlight, and it was clear that the woman wasn't dressed for hiking. She wore a bright purple ankle-length dress and a matching purple floral scarf.

Slowing next to a tree, she pressed her hand to the bark and smiled sadly. She whispered words that were too soft for Finn to hear and knelt by the tree. From her messenger bag, she picked up a spade and started digging. After a few minutes, she reached in, pulled out a jar, and placed it in the hole. When she covered the hole, she stood and looked at the moon. Raising her hands, she whispered a few more words, wrapped the shawl tighter around her shoulders, and disappeared back into the forest.

"What is that?" Zane asked as he stood.

"A spell jar." Finn walked over to the hole and began sifting through the dirt.

"And you're stealing it?"

"I am." Finn looked up at the werewolf with a grin. "That woman is rumored to be one of the women sleeping with Darren, and as far as I know, she's not a witch, so if she's performing a little magic, I sure as hell want to know why."

CHAPTER 18
FINN

The door wouldn't open.

Which would have been fine if it was locked, but Finn hadn't already locked the door. The knob turned just fine.

The door still didn't open.

When he put his shoulder into it, the door growled at him.

"All right," Finn muttered. "Come on. You're mad at me? I've only been gone for a couple of hours. It's not like I abandoned you."

He tried again, but the manor didn't budge. The door was practically sealed.

"Behave, or I'll turn your backyard into a pool."

The door grumbled again but reluctantly swung open. Finn shook his head and pushed it open. He could still feel the house giving him the cold shoulder. Just what had gotten it so upset?

Kicking off his shoes, he stepped onto the front rug and yelped.

Cold and wet.

Sugar. That little demon. After trying to eat him all afternoon, apparently, he'd peed on the foyer rug. No wonder the house was mad.

"He's not even my dog!"

No response. Shaking his head, he headed to the kitchen, grabbed a towel and cleaner, and cleaned up the mess. When he headed back to the kitchen, the light was on, and Paris stood, blinking blearily at him. "You're home."

Home. He had a strange mix of feelings hearing that word. Coming from her. At the same time, she was standing there like she'd just rolled out of bed.

"I am. Did I wake you up?"

"I was only half asleep."

She looked troubled. Sitting the stolen jar on the table, he gave her his full attention. "Dinner with Annie, go okay?"

"Dinner with Annie turned out to be dinner with Annie and a third of Helena's coven. They expect me to take control now that I have my magic." She ran her hands over her face. "I just got my magic. I can't even light a candle, and now they want me to balance the magic in Silver Mist? Some of them knew my mother. They knew she had magic. They remembered when she practiced magic. She had it as a child, but I'm forty-two, Finn! I'm just now getting my magic! Why did it take me this long? What did Helena say about me to make them think I'd be remotely capable of heading a coven!"

The more she spoke, the higher her voice went. Finn reached out and pulled her in for a hug. Wrapping her hands around him, she buried her head in his shoulder and squeezed. Slowly, he stroked her hair. "A lot is happening to you, Paris. You don't owe anyone any answers. You don't have to make any decisions. Just get to know your magic. Develop your relationship with it. Then you can worry about everything else."

She raised her head and stared at him. "I can feel your heartbeat, Finn. It's beating awfully fast."

"Maybe I just like it when you hug me."

"Or maybe you know something that you aren't telling me." Dropping her arms, she stepped back. "That's alright. I'll get your secrets out of you. What is that?"

For a moment, he'd forgotten about the jar. Picking it up, he studied. "It's something that I shouldn't have. Someone else's spell jar."

"Okay. So, who does it belong to, and why do you have it."

Finn explained what happened. Paris started making some tea, and by the time they sat at the table, there were two steaming cups in front of them. "Finn. That seems like huge magic. Pulling that from nature decades later? Why aren't you the head of the coven?"

"We all have our talents, and leading is definitely not mine."

"I made an appointment with Annabelle's son. I'm getting a personal reading from her tomorrow. I thought maybe I could get my own questions in then. My questioning of Marsha didn't go so well."

She filled him in while he studied the jar. "Dana," Finn sighed. "I'm sorry Ginger ran into her. Dana has never liked her for some reason."

"So you're going to study the jar."

"I need to open it safely first. Since Annabelle is not a witch, it's not likely to be a very powerful spell jar. I can tell she made it herself. Her grief is written all over it."

"She's grieving, Darren," Paris said softly. It was clear

she felt conflicted about that. Finn could see she still had such a big heart, but she was so certain that Darren was someone who had hurt her. It was hard to grieve his death.

"My magic is mostly with the living earth. Dried herbs don't really speak to me. Once I open the seal, the spell will be released. If it's as mundane as I suspect, we won't even feel it, but if I'm wrong, I could release something."

"Could I try?"

Despite being bombarded by Annie and the coven, she wasn't shying away from her magic. Helena knew that she would be a strong witch, but that part of that strength came from being a strong person. Finn always knew she was that.

"Come here." Standing up, he pushed the chair back and waited for her to round the table. "Place your hands on the jar."

When she cupped the jar, he stood behind her and placed his hands on hers. "Focus on the jar. There's magic within the glass, but there's also so much emotion in it. Close your eyes and focus on that inner strength. Open yourself and feel."

She shivered just a little, and for a moment, he thought he felt a spark between them. An actual spark of magic converging. "I can feel it," Paris whispered. "So much pain. Sadness. Oh, this poor woman."

"There's a seal on the jar. It's meant to keep the magic in. You can crack the wax with your magic, but you have to be careful. Be ready to sense and deactivate any magic that escapes."

Paris looked up at him and wrinkled her nose. "I'm going to need more instructions than just crack the wax with your magic."

"Just like with the candle. Picture in your mind and

funnel your magic into that small area. Like a hammer. Your magic is that hammer."

"Okay."

"Keep your body loose. This magic is yours to command. The easiest thing in the world. It's like thumping something with your finger, only it's with your magic. Breathe and..."

The glass shattered. Paris jumped but didn't shriek. "Oh, no. What have I done? I didn't feel anything. I didn't feel a spell."

"It's okay. That's because there was nothing to feel. No spell. Just Annabelle's grief. Either someone sold her a dud, which is likely in this town, or she tried the spell herself. How do you feel?"

"A little shaky," she admitted. "I should get this glass cleaned up."

"Let me do that. Drink your tea."

Finn cleaned up the glass and rejoined her. "I think I might have hammered my magic a little too hard," she said wryly.

"Control comes with practice and experience, Paris. You have a lot of power. It takes time to learn to control that. You've only had days. Give yourself a break. You're doing very well."

Smiling a little, Paris sipped her tea. "You didn't expect to be teaching me magic when you came to Silver Mist."

"No, but then, you were always very unexpected."

"So what do you see in the jar, and how does it help us?"

"Annabelle poured her grief into this jar, so it has some-thing to do with Darren." Most of it was finely chopped and pulverized herbs and difficult to identify, but there were some full leaves and twigs. Some flowers. "This is a forget-me-not, which is mostly used in memory spells. It's not like whatever messed with your memory. It's more like an emotional memory of how you feel connected to a memory. This is an orchid flower, which is...odd. Bark off an elderberry."

"And apple slices," Paris said as she leaned over the table. "What kind of spell uses apple slices?"

"There are a lot of different uses for apples. Fertility spells. Power boosts. They're not good for long-lasting spells, though, like jar spells. The apples rot." Confused, he sorted through the ingredients. "I can't think of any spells that would combine all of these items, but I can think of something they all have in common."

"What's that?"

"They're meant to attract the Fae."

"Fae? Why would Annabelle need that?"

Finn shook his head. "I have no idea."

NERVOUS ABOUT HER READING, Paris headed to Annabelle's shop early. She'd planned to walk around the other shops for a little bit and work off some nervous energy, but when she saw Annabelle in the window, working on her display, she headed straight in.

Annabelle turned to greet her and, just like her son, stopped and studied her quietly. Finally, she offered a smile." Liam was right about you. New to your craft but powerful. Threads of heartbreak in your past, tightly woven together to create strength for a weighty destiny."

The urge to turn and flee tugged at her, but Paris swallowed hard. "Your son recognized me, and you did some reading."

"My son was smart enough to realize that you are not a Sarah Brown, but he doesn't know who you are. I didn't know who you were until you walked into my shop, but I had been expecting you. I know you want to ask me questions. Let me do your reading, and then I will answer any question I can for you about Darren."

So much for catching Annabelle off guard; now it was Paris who was unsteady on her feet. It was easier to go through with the reading when she thought Annabelle was a fake. As much as Paris wanted to know the truth about her past, she was much more hesitant to know about her future.

"It's all right. I can't tell you specifics. I can't tell you if the man you're yearning for is going to be your happily ever after or if you're going to patch up your relationship with your friends. I can see many paths emanating from you. The one you choose is up to you."

"You loved him."

"Reading first," Annabelle admonished, although her eyes grew a little wet. "Then you may ask about Darren."

"I didn't drink the tea."

"For you, it won't matter."

Reluctantly, Paris nodded, and Annabelle flipped the lock and pulled out a sign that read *Currently in a Reading. Please return at...*

She scribbled in a time and hung the sign on the door. "Now nobody will disturb us. Follow me."

Behind the curtain, literally, was a small closed-off room. No windows or overhead lights, but enough atmospheric lighting for Paris to find her way to a cushioned bench. Folding up her legs, she leaned against the pillows and intertwined her fingers nervously. Annabelle sat on a matching bench on the other side of a small room. Around them were lovely green plants, although Paris couldn't figure out how they lived without sunlight, crystals, and a few amulets. There was no crystal ball or tarot cards. No table to do a palm reading.

"You read auras." Like her son.

"Yes, in the most simplified version. I read energy that's attached to people, the energy that they emanate, and, in very rare cases, the energy that's waiting to be consumed. Those cases are for people with unavoidable destinies."

"Like me."

"Yes. You and your friends were forever tied to the magical community before you even knew what it was. It's unfair, but there isn't much you can do about it, unfortunately. Are you ready to begin?"

"What do I have to do?"

"Nothing. Your aura is bright enough to be seen under a brilliantly clear noonday. Just try and be comfortable."

Easier said than done. Paris shifted a little bit and was reminded about all the times Helena tried to get her to meditate. When she focused on being relaxed, she just got more tense. Finally, she gave up and smiled forcefully at Annabelle.

"You were born in darkness. I don't mean that literally, of course. I mean that the things that would be most important to you were hidden away, and although many people tried to unlock your magic, no one told you the truth. You are confused by that. Even a little bitter." When Paris scowled, Annabelle laughed. "It's not a judgment, my dear. Just an observation. In your shoes, I imagine I would be bitter as well.

"When you were taken, your world shrank. Those days shaped who you are now and who you will become but in many different ways. You are right that what happened to you then is important, and you should know the truth, but what you do know, the effect that it had on the town, is important as well. You should know that it's not all their fault."

At that, Paris straightened. "Excuse me? They called us liars and shunned us. Helena never spoke to me again!"

"The days that you disappeared, the town changed. A shift in energy so strong that even the humans felt it," Annabelle said softly. "I moved here after it happened, and until recently, I didn't know what it was like. I just know what I saw in people's aura. A strange suppression that I had never seen anywhere else. In the last few days, everyone is so much brighter. It was like a weight lifted off their shoulders."

"You're saying I did something to them?"

"I don't know, dear. I just know that something happened that made them very uncomfortable. When that happens, people have to explain it somehow. I imagine you were their best targets."

"Helena knew. She didn't need to blame me."

"I can't speak for Helena. I can only tell you what I see in you, and you did very well for yourself. You were alone and felt even more alone, but you tapped into your spiritual side even if you didn't know it. Built a business on it."

"I'm a designer. I mean, I'm good at it, but I wouldn't say I use any magic for it. I didn't even have my magic then."

Pursing her lips, Annabelle studied her and shook her head. "You're wrong, my dear. So was I. You've had your magic for a very long time. I can see old roots running through you. Strong but unused."

Angry, Paris stood. Now, she was just making up things, and for what? The drama? Annabelle had real abilities. She'd expected more from the woman. "No. I would know if I had magic."

"Would you? You didn't even know magic existed until you moved back. This isn't Harry Potter, dear. You aren't going to make things disappear accidentally or conjure things with a simple thought. Magic requires practice. Intent."

"But I could see things after the earthquake. Things I couldn't see before," Paris argued. "That was obviously my magic unlocking itself. I think this reading is over."

Annabelle nodded. "All right. I won't continue without your consent. I promised you that I would answer your questions. You may go ahead."

All Paris wanted to do was run. She couldn't even conceive a life where she'd had magic all along but couldn't access it. To know that Helena had abandoned her even when she did have magic, but Annabelle was telling the truth about everything else. Paris knew it.

Was she telling the truth about this?

It didn't matter. That wasn't her primary goal. She was there for answers about Darren. She wasn't leaving without them.

"You were having an affair with the man who kidnapped me."

Annabelle's eyes widened, and guilt sliced through Paris. She'd been so certain that Annabelle had known. Wasn't that why Annabelle was so free with her reading? Curiosity?

"I'm sorry," the psychic told her finally with trembling hands. "I didn't know."

"Really? You could see all this about me, but you couldn't see his past?"

"I can only see what's visible to me. Some beings have the power to hide. You do as well, although I gather you don't know how to do that yet. I can teach you if you wish."

"Darren."

Nodding, she took a deep breath. "Yes. First, you should know that I was not having an affair. My husband and I are in the middle of a quiet divorce. We've been separated for over a year, and the divorce will be final next month. He is also seeing someone. It's amicable, but we're keeping everything quiet for Liam. He knows about the divorce, but we were hoping to avoid gossip. Obviously, we were not quite enough. Darren and I had been dating for almost six months. We loved each other."

"You're sure about that?"

"Love is the one energy that can't be hidden. Your feelings are front and center. Anger toward me. Betrayal toward Helena. And love, although I can only speculate who that is for. Darren's love for me was in his aura. It was there, and it was true."

"Did you know he had secrets?"

"Yes. There were parts of his aura that he was actively keeping from me. Things in his past. I didn't think much about it. We all have done things that we want to keep hidden."

"But he's human. How could he hide parts of his aura from you? Was someone helping him?"

Annabelle looked down at her hands. When she didn't say anything, Paris went to her. "Annabelle, you said you would answer everything that you could. Who was helping Darren? It's okay if you don't know."

"As far as I know, Darren didn't have help. He didn't need it. Darren wasn't human."

"He wasn't?" That didn't make sense. If Darren wasn't human, wouldn't the other witches have known it? No one had said anything about it. She thought about the ingredients in the jar. "He's fae. I don't...nobody said anything.

Does no one know? How could he have hidden that here of all places?"

"When we started dating, I also thought he was human, but there was something about his aura I couldn't identify. I tried to do some research on it, but most of the books written by aura readers aren't authentic, and of course, there's no book on the fae aura. In time, he admitted to me that he was a very rare species. He was orphaned at a young age, and outside of his family, he'd never met another like himself. He's excellent at glamour, even to those with the magical sight."

"Did he tell you what kind?"

"No," Annabelle shook her head. "And I never asked. It seemed rude."

"Do you know what kind of gifts he had?"

"No. If he used them, it was never in my presence."

Nodding, Paris stood. "I know this is hard for you. I can tell that you loved him, and it hurts to discover those we love keeping things from us. Believe me, I know. Is there anything else you think I should know? I need to find out what happened to me, Annabelle. You said so yourself. It's important."

"It is," Annabelle sighed. "And for more than just you. I can't shake the feeling that the town's future resides in you discovering the truth. I can tell you that I have seen an aura similar to Darren's in one other resident in town. I never asked, but I firmly believe that Darren has a brother."

CHAPTER 19
PARIS

Darren had a brother.

It was easy to latch on to that rather than think about anything else the psychic had told her. Silver Mist Cove had its fair share of frauds or rather showmen, but Annabelle was clearly not one of them. Still, she had to be wrong. Paris hadn't had her magic for forever. That was something she should have been able to feel, right?

Pushing that aside, she focused on something that was easier to swallow. Darren had a brother. Anthony Peterman.

Two different last names, and from what Paris could tell, no one else had made the connection. It was possible that Annabelle was mistaken. Maybe they just happened to be the only two species of their kind in town but weren't related.

Although, if that were the case, wouldn't they at least be friends? Have some kind of connection? They had to know.

Annabelle had told her that Anthony owned a hardware

147

store but was also one of the big draws to the main stage. The hardware store was just a few blocks from Annabelle's store, so Paris walked and allowed herself to be absorbed into the town.

It hadn't occurred to her before how many secrets Silver Mist Cove was hiding. There were some diehard fans who came, believing the psychics, but most came knowing that it was all flair and drama. It hadn't occurred to Paris that the clear veneer of deception on the town actually hid real secrets and lies.

The creatures who lived here weren't just in hiding from humans. They were in hiding from each other.

Everyone has secrets, my dear. What you see is never what you get.

Helena's words rang so clearly in her head that Paris stumbled, but it was a memory. When she'd been twelve, the winter in Silver Mist had been particularly brutal. She'd left on her bike around noon to hang out with Sage, but her friend hadn't been at her meeting spot. Desperately needing some warmth and wondering if her friend had forgotten, she'd gone to the bar. It was a Sunday and closed, but she went through the back entrance like she'd always done with Sage.

Only Sage hadn't been there. Jack, her father, has been standing over the gas logs in the dining area and feeding something into the flames. There was something that had caught her attention, something that had mesmerized her about him, and she just quietly stared. Thinking back, Paris didn't know what it was, but when Jack had whipped his head around, his eyes were blazed in a fury of gold.

He'd thundered at her and scared her so bad that she'd run out, hopped on her bike, and pedaled home as fast as she could. Helena was waiting for her. Jack had already called to apologize for scaring her and making sure that she'd made it home.

When Paris tried to explain that something hadn't felt right at the bar, Helena had only gently reminded her that she'd entered his sacred space and didn't have the right to judge him.

Since she'd come back, she found nothing but secrets. Most, she'd understood and delighted in.

Now, she wondered if everyone was keeping secrets. Had Helena been hiding something from Paris? Something other than her witchcraft?

"Hey, Paris. Everything okay?"

Startled, she jerked her head. Someone had fallen into step with her, and she hadn't even noticed.

"Deputy Dash. Are you on your morning rounds?" Knowing what she knew now, she couldn't help but peek at him with her witch eyes. Finn had said that the sheriff's station knew about magical and magical creatures. Did that mean no one who worked there was Herman? Dash's appearance was still very human, so he either was human, in the know, and maybe there were plenty of them, or he was a witch. It was rude to ask, she knew, and dangerous.

"Technically, I'm always on duty, but in this case, I'm leaving the night shift. I had breakfast with some friends, and now I'm heading home to crash for a few hours. Night work is brutal on my sleep schedule."

"Is there always someone available at night?"

"One of the deputies always works as a night dispatcher. It's pretty boring, but that's a good thing."

"Is it?"

"Sure. That means there are no emergencies, and I get to catch up on my shows. That is, of course, unless someone finds a dead body in their home, but that's rare. Seems to only happen once in a decade."

Paris chuckled at the jesting accusation in his voice. "It's not my fault! I promise, Deputy Dash, that this is the first dead body that I've ever found."

"Sure, but it's not your first Silver Mist Cove emergency, is it?"

His voice was light, but Paris's stomach tightened. Dash glanced over and sighed. "Oh, man. I'm sorry. I shouldn't have said anything. I'm really not one of those people who blame you for what happened all those years ago. I guess no matter how much time has passed, it's still not okay to joke about it."

"I think Ginger, Sage, and I are always going to be a little touchy on the subject."

"Ginger is back in town? I didn't know that. Are you sure?"

At the urgency of his voice, she frowned. "I am certain. I've seen her a couple of times."

"Sorry. It's my job to know what is happening in this town. I don't like it when things slip by me."

Still matching his pace, Paris turned and raised her eyebrows. "Is that really all you're worried about?"

His cheeks grew pink. "Of course. I'm turning here."

Ah. So Deputy Dash had a little crush on Ginger. That was cute. Maybe Paris would tell her friend. Dash might have been a little older than them, but he was a good-looking man.

"Oh, before you go, I have a question for you. The file on my disappearance is really thin. Do you think the sheriff would be open to me talking with him about it? Maybe help me fill in some gaps? I know how he feels about it."

"The Sheriff let you look at the file? Good for him. If I'm

being honest, I think he feels a little guilty about how he handled things. He was just a young deputy, and we've all done things in our past we aren't proud of."

He could make up for it by being nice to her now, but Paris didn't point that out. He had, after all, given her the file. That was something.

"You deserve some closure, although I've seen the file myself, and I know what you mean. I don't know how much the sheriff can help you, but maybe he can give you the number for Sheriff Mills. I think he moved to Florida after he retired. He might know more."

"Thanks. I'll be sure to ask. I hope you get some sleep."

"Me too." He gave her a little salute and turned off to a small neighborhood. Paris walked another block and then turned to the hardware store.

After a few trips around the store, Paris surmised that Anthony wasn't in. There were two young teenagers manning the counter, but there was a sign next to the register that caught her interest.

Showtimes for Anthony the Amazing. His next show was tomorrow.

If he was hiding his relationship with his brother, the only way she might get some answers was to take him by surprise.

Ambushing him after his show? Hard to hide the real things that mattered when you were focused on putting on a show.

THE FINAL DETAILS of Helena's funeral were finished. Sitting in his car, staring up at the house, Finn couldn't help but feel that there was nothing left to do but feel her absence. During his formative years, she was such a big part of her life, but this past year, he'd been taking care of her. Making sure she was keeping to her doctor appointments instead of just relying on her magic to heal herself. Paying landscapers to take care of her lawn because she couldn't handle much more than her garden. Keeping an eye on her finances so she didn't fall prey to any scams.

So much of it was done over the phone and over video chats once she learned how. Maybe if he'd taken the time to see her more than once or twice a year, he would see that she was having health problems.

Although when he did come to visit, he watched her. While she cooked, when she gardened, even when she cast and used most of her energy. Nothing stood out to him or worried him.

Hard to believe she'd had a heart attack.

As he got out of the car, he couldn't help but feel the darkness settle back inside of him. After all those years of her telling him that Paris wasn't for him, that she was destined for great things while Finn would hardly make a dent in the magic world, why would she throw him back in her path like this? Give the house to both of them?

It was like a taunt from beyond the grave, although, despite his resentment, he knew that Helena wasn't the type to taunt. She was straightforward and sometimes callously honest, but she didn't go out of her way to be cruel.

He went inside intent on grabbing a snack for dinner and holing up in his room when a sharp bark followed by the aroma of savory chicken caught his attention.

Chicken and cheese.

"Oh, good. You're home. I wasn't sure when you'd get back, and I didn't want your nachos to get cold, but I was famished."

Paris was at the stove in a thin yellow dress and a pink apron that said *Kiss the Cook* on it. No doubt it was conjured by the house because Finn had never seen it before.

Since he did very much want to kiss the cook, he tore his eyes from the apron and forced a smile. Sugar snapped at his ankles, helping to break the spell. "Nachos, huh?"

"Just something easy to throw together. I was getting ready to make a salad." She twisted her fingers in front of her. "Is that all right? Is it weird that I was taking you into account when making dinner plans? I know we're living together for the moment, but I guess we don't have to eat together."

"It's fine. Thoughtful, even. Let me just take a few minutes to change, and I'll join you."

That bright smile was instantly back on her face. "Great. I wanted to talk to you about what Annabelle said and let you know what my next move was."

With a short nod, he went upstairs and closed his eyes. The funeral was in a few days. Afterward, there would be no real reason for him to stay. The dead body wasn't his responsibility. Paris's mission is to discover the truth about her missing days. Also, it's not his responsibility.

His only job was to put Helena's spirit to rest. If he had any decency, he would tell Paris that tonight.

Changing into some lounge pants and a tee-shirt, he headed downstairs to a barking Sugar. The small white chubster growled at him with all the fury in his little body, but when Finn reached down to pat him on the head, Sugar surprisingly quieted. Maybe they were becoming friends, or maybe the little maniac was conserving energy for a late-night attack. Last night, after getting up to pee, the little rodent had tripped him right on top of the steps. Finn still couldn't believe that it was an accident. The dog probably had a body count.

He walked into the kitchen, unsurprised to find the candles fully lit on the table, but Paris and the food were not there.

"Finn? I'm in the living room. I hope that's okay."

Joining her in the living room, he couldn't help but grin. Nothing romantic in that room. The house rumbled a little in annoyance.

"Stop that," Paris said, tapping her foot on the carpet. "It has been a long and trying day, and I want to relax on the couch and eat. The table looks very nice, but it's a little too formal for what I need right now."

"You eat wherever you want to eat. The couch actually seems great. Why was your day long and trying? Annabelle, say some things that upset you?"

"Something like that." Her eyes widened as she put a couple of plates down, and she reached into her pocket and pulled out her phone. "Oh, it's Ginger. She wants Sage and I to have dinner with her tomorrow night. Is that all right?"

"You don't have to run your plans by me."

His words were shorter than he meant, and she pocketed her phone. "What did you do today?"

"Finished finalizing Helena's funeral plans."

"Oh, Finn, I'm so sorry. Maybe we should put everything aside and just enjoy dinner and relax."

His dark mood grew. "No, let's talk about the investigation. It'll be a good way to take my mind off things."

So much for not getting even more involved. Maybe tomorrow.

CHAPTER 20
FINN

There was a warm body pressed against him. Finn moved just a little, and the woman shifted and tossed her arm over his chest. He knew who it was without opening his eyes. There was only one woman he'd have in his bed these days, but Paris wasn't in his bed. They weren't in any bed.

Cracking open his eyes, he squinted as bright light streamed through the windows. He was stiff from sleeping in one position all night. There's not a lot of room on the couch.

One arm around Paris, he looked down at her and smiled. Her golden hair was spread out all over his chest and the back of the couch. Her mouth was open, and she snored like a trucker. Perched on top of her butt, Sugar glared at him as if it was Finn's fault that the dog didn't have Paris all to himself.

They'd talked until late. She'd been certain that Annabelle wasn't a fake, but it didn't make sense to her that she'd had her magic all her life. It agitated her so much that Finn had pulled her into his lap and held her.

It hadn't made sense to him either. Helena had waited for years for Paris to come into her magic. Why would she keep it a secret? There was no way that Paris had her magic, and Helena didn't know. Even if Paris had been halfway across the world, Helena would have known.

Quietly, he reminded her that Annabelle had a reason to lie. She'd been dating Darren. What if she just wanted to distract Paris?

Paris responded with words of wisdom from Helena. Everyone was hiding something. They'd talked about Helena until she fell asleep. Unwilling to move her, he'd let her sleep until he slipped into sleep as well.

Now, his body was paying for it, but he had zero regrets.

With a snort, the snoring stopped, and Paris moved and opened her eyes. "Easy," he murmured. "Don't fall off."

Her eyes widened, and she lifted her head. He saw the moment she realized where she was and who she was with, but she didn't jerk away. "Good morning," she murmured huskily. "Am I too heavy for you?"

"Never."

Smiling sleepily, she shifted just a little, falling to the back of the couch and curling her leg up against him. She never lost eye contact. "You feel better?"

"What do you mean?"

"I could see that you were upset last night." She placed a hand on his chest. "You miss Helena."

"Hmm. I was upset last night."

"You don't feel better." Disappointment shadowed her face. "What can I do, Finn?"

She was doing it just by being with him. She was chasing away the shadows and filling him with hope for a future that Helena had dashed to pieces.

"I need a shower and to get some work done," he said as he shifted and moved out from under her. "I know you're going to speak to Anthony today. Can you wait for me, and we'll go together?"

When she stood, she sat upright and pushed her hair out of her face. "Finn, what are we doing here?"

"I told you, I have to get a little work done."

"No." Taking Sugar in her arms, she stroked his head and took a deep breath. "I mean, what are the two of us doing? I had such a crush growing up with you, and now that you're back in my life, I realize that those feelings are still there. There's chemistry here, but you keep backing away. Do you feel it? Is it in my head?"

The mask was gone, and in the early morning sunlight, she looked at him with such vulnerability. Everything she felt was in her eyes as she stared at him with such hope.

He couldn't lie to her.

"I do feel it, Paris," he told her regretfully. "With Helena's death, old feelings are cropping up. We're living together and..."

"No." She shook her head. "Don't play this off as circumstances. Please. If you don't have any feelings for me, just say so."

"It's not that easy, Paris. Whatever we feel for each other, the future is going to have other plans. There are very different paths for us."

"What do you mean? Because we live in different cities? That isn't something you think we can work around?"

"No. I mean, magically. Paris. Magically, we're on two different levels."

As soon as he said the words, he knew he'd made a mistake. The mask slammed back in place, but he saw the flash of emotion.

Pain.

"I've said something to hurt you. I'm sorry. That was never my intention. I just meant —"

"It's fine," she cut in. "I understand. You don't need to worry about my feelings, Finn. I'm a big girl. I'm just glad that we cleared the air. Now, I can focus on my investigation. I'm going to take a shower. Sorry, I think I drooled on you. You know, when the funeral is done, we should figure out what to do with all of this. I can sell you my half if you can afford it. Just think about it. There's probably nothing really here for me anyway."

Her voice was flat as she combed her hands through her hair. Finn watched, helpless, as she held Sugar close and practically fled up the stairs.

"Women are complex creatures, Finn. You need to handle them with care."

"Hindsight, Aunt Helena," he muttered. "More current advice would be helpful."

There was no answer.

THE AMAZING ANTHONY was not a psychic. It was a magician's act and a very impressive one. For a moment, Paris forgot what she was doing there when she watched him rise into the air. His assistant passed swords over and under him, demonstrating that there were no wires. The crowd, a large one for Silver Mist, considering that it wasn't the height of tourist season, went wild.

Paris relaxed just a little and couldn't help but get swept away to a time when she was a naive child of Silver Mist. She'd sit with Ginger and Sage and watch Ginger's mother perform. Her psychic routine included a few acrobatic moves that left the more conservative members of the town gasping with outrage. They, however, loved it. For a whole year, they practiced to try and mimic the routine, but only Ginger came even close to mirroring it.

When it looked like the show was about to wind down, Paris made her way to the side entrance and slipped through the doors. There was never any security outside of the summer hours, and since she knew the theater well, it was easy to get to the dressing rooms. There were two side-by-side, both the same size. A quick peak in the first one told her that it was Anthony's assistant, so she slipped into the second one and waited.

Nervous, her mind wandered as the seconds ticked by. Unfortunately, it flashed back to the morning and her humiliating conversation with Finn.

How could she be so stupid? It hadn't even occurred to her that Finn would care about their difference in magical levels. Naturally, Finn would be better at it. He'd been wielding magic his whole life, and Paris had only learned of her a few weeks ago. She was getting better, but it would be years until she was on Finn's level.

Maybe he'd want her then.

When did Finn even care about magic? His job wasn't magical. He didn't live in Silver Mist. For all that she knew, no one he worked with or was friends with even knew that he was a witch. Why was it so important to him?

Maybe it was Helena's upbringing. Maybe she'd instilled witch snobbery in him.

Or maybe he really wasn't interested in her, and that was the only thing he could come up with to let her down gently.

Either way, it stung.

The door opened, and Paris jerked to attention. It slammed shut, and she stepped around the costumes. "Mr.

Peterman, please don't be alarmed. I just have some questions for you."

He was in the process of taking off his robe when he caught sight of Paris. "You."

"Oh. Well, I was going to introduce myself, but it's clear you already know who I am. Strange because until yesterday, I didn't know who you were."

"Everyone knows who you are," Anthony said flatly. To her surprise, he made no move to exit the dressing room. "What are you doing here?"

She spoke quickly before she lost him. "I have questions about the dead body found in Helena's house. Darren."

There was a brief flicker of pain before he schooled his features. "I don't know him."

"He's your brother."

This time, it was more than a flicker. Anthony's eyes widened. Paris thought he was going to deny it, but then his shoulders slumped. "Nobody knows that."

She had him. No way he was going to leave now or threaten to call security. Now, she just had to hope that he didn't lie to her. "The woman that Darren was seeing can read auras. She can see the magic in auras. Darren's was special. She said yours was the same. If it makes you feel better, I don't think she told anyone, and Darren never shared it with her."

"Annabelle," Anthony murmured. "I suppose I should reach out to her, but Darren and I...it was complicated."

"Complicated or not, I'm sorry about your loss. Whatever your current relationship was with him, he was your brother. You must have been close if you'd moved here together."

Anthony sighed as he removed his robe. Underneath, he wore a pair of grey cotton shorts and a tee shirt. "Adrien and I used to be so close when we were teenagers. When we found out what we were, our fae heritage, it divided us." His voice grew bitter as if he wanted nothing to do with what he was. Paris couldn't help but wonder if many children felt the same when they found out. Had Sage? There was still so much she didn't know about the woman who'd been one of her best friends.

"I wanted to hide, and he wanted to embrace it. Ironically, I was the one who moved to a safe haven first. I got into a local college and moved here. It was strange. Everyone was in hiding but also out. It was freeing in an odd kind of way. Then, Adrien showed up, but he wasn't using his real name."

"Did he know that you were here?"

"He did. He said that he saw an opportunity for us to make some money. Together. Taking advantage of the tourism business. Our father was a thief and a con artist. Adrien wanted to follow in his footsteps. I didn't want anything to do with it, but I promised that as long as he kept his distance, I wouldn't out him. I was the one who pushed him away."

Paris shook her head. "I don't buy it. You lived in the same town for decades and didn't try to repair your relationship?"

Anthony ran his hand through his hair and shook his head. Tears filled his eyes. "For the first two years, we didn't speak. We didn't even acknowledge each other on the street. Then, something happened. He came to me one night and said he'd gotten in over his head. He'd made a terrible mistake, and he needed my help to fix it. I refused. Whatever he was involved with, I didn't even want to know. I sent him away again. The only regret I have in my life."

"That had to be a long time ago, Anthony."

"Yeah, and maybe it was for the best. He got himself out. He got back on his own two feet. Started a business. Stopped thieving. A couple of years ago, we both ended up at Jack's bar. I just couldn't do it anymore. I couldn't be a stranger. I'd just gone through a break-up, and, well, you don't care about anything about that. I started up a conversation, and it felt good. We never became what we used to be. We saw each other maybe once a month. He'd have me over for dinner, or I'd have him over. Sometimes we met for drinks. The last time I saw him was a week before his death. He said he wanted me to meet Annabelle. He was in love."

Sitting on the bench, Anthony knocked his head back against the wall. "Someone came into the shop, gossiping about his death. It was the first I'd ever heard of it. I wanted to go to the sheriff to demand information, but I'd kept Adrien's secret for years. Called him Darren. Hid all his sins. I was worried it would come back on me if I said anything. I can't even claim his body."

Seeing his pain, Paris sat next to him and took his hand. "Annabelle is going through her divorce, but she was in love with Darren. Sorry, Adrien. She knows about you, and I think she'll help you keep his secret. You can claim his body through her, have him buried."

"Not under his real name."

"No, but he's been living as Darren much longer than he was living as Adrien. Maybe Darren was the man who was always meant to be. Someone who chased a dream only to discover he was someone else altogether."

"You're awfully kind to him, especially considering what happened."

"What do you mean?"

Anthony sighed and looked her in the eye. "The night

he came to, talking about making a huge mistake and needing a way out? It was the same night that you and your friends appeared in the woods with no memory."

Paris swallowed hard. She knew that Darren had been involved, but it was something else altogether to have someone else make the connection. "Did he give you any specifics?"

"No, and believe me, if he did, I would tell you. I saw this town turn on you. It was difficult to watch, but that's what fear does. Everyone knew something horrible had happened, but no one wanted to admit it. I think they still don't want to admit it. I didn't help. I could have gotten the truth from Darren. That will be my sin."

If he was looking for forgiveness, Paris couldn't give it to him. She still needed answers. Then, maybe she could start forgiving people for what they did. Or, in his case, what they didn't do. "You and Darren are a rare type of fae, right?"

"Yes." Anthony reached up and waved a hand over his eyes. Instantly, they were milky white, but when he looked at her, she knew that he hadn't lost his vision. He was just looking at her from a different point of view. "We can see your memories."

Immediately, Paris stumbled away. "Can you do more than see them?" She whispered.

"Yes. We can remove them."

CHAPTER 21

PARIS

Paris was shaken after seeing Anthony, and the last thing she wanted to do was see Finn. Fortunately, whatever business he had kept him in his room, so she was able to sneak in, grab Sugar, and sneak back out again. Needing to kill a couple of hours before her dinner with the girls, she also grabbed one of the books that was in Helena's library and headed out to the forest.

It was a spell book, hidden away in her library among the many other books she'd collected over the years. Paris had found it the night before when she couldn't sleep. She probably should have given it to Finn, but she just wanted to absorb magic, to learn everything she could about it.

She'd give it to him, eventually, and she wouldn't try anything that seemed dangerous. She certainly wouldn't be performing any more spells on people. She'd learned her lesson.

Standing on the edge, she stared into the woods. Up until the event, she'd loved playing in the woods. She, Sage, and Ginger had played hide and seek as children. As teenagers, they'd snuck a few boyfriends into the woods to make out. No matter what, she always felt drawn to the mists that cascaded out from the heart of the woods.

One day, she planned on exploring to discover just where those mists came from. She'd never gotten around to it.

Now, all she could feel was panic.

"It's all right, Sugar. These spells are specifically nature spells. That means I need to be in nature to cast them. Being on the edge of nature probably counts. There's dirt under my feet and blue skies over me."

Sugar sat and sneezed. Paris sighed. "You're right. It's just a bunch of trees. Nothing to be scared of. I can do this."

Still, she stared. Sugar sneezed again, and Paris sighed and sat. "Maybe I should review the spells before I march into the middle of nowhere and start casting." The grass started tickling her skin as she opened the book. Unlike the other books, this one looked hardbound. The spine bindings were uneven, and the glue was coming undone, but the pages weren't old. Curious, she studied the first page.

"*Natural Night Magic,*" she murmured. "By Finn Whitlock."

Based on the handwriting, Paris imagined that Finn was young when he wrote it. The spelling was a little bit off, and the handwriting was shaky. She couldn't help but smile. Helena must have bound this for him.

So little Finn had come up with his own magical spells. No wonder he thought they were on a different level magically. "Looks like I don't have to go in the woods today after all. These spells are for nighttime."

Carefully, so she didn't damage any of the pages, she flipped through the book. Paris didn't have any idea what constituted high-level magic, but she was impressed by the spells. Almost all of it was plant-based, although it was clear that Finn had been experimenting with crystals as well. Like math class, the book kept all of his work, showing Finn's excitement when something worked and the bold strikes through the things that didn't.

"How to hide my lite brite. How to make vegetables disappear. Protection spells for my treehouse." Paris read with a giggle. Clearly, Finn had his priorities in order.

The more she flipped through the pages, the more the spells changed. Matured. Paris whistled. Helena must have collected Finn's spells throughout the years. The magic became more confident. They seemed to require less groundwork to make them work. *"Spells to be cool around girls,"* Paris read and shook her head. Finn had always been confident. Strange to think he thought he'd needed magic.

Some of them seemed complex. Other medicinal. Lowering high blood pressure. Easing arthritis. They were not things that Finn had to deal with.

Helena? Was he trying to help her?

Turning the page, her hand stilled.

The page was just called Paris.

Trembling, she traced her name with her finger before turning the page. And another. And another. Fifteen pages total, all dedicated to her.

There were likes and dislikes. Raisins. She hadn't liked raisins since she was very young. It must have been why he'd crossed it out with a different colored ink. In one corner, hastily scribbled, was a peace spell. It was dated.

August. She'd been around fourteen. It was the summer Danny Hiskins had broken up with her after they'd been hot and heavy for two weeks, or at least as hot and heavy as fourteen-year-olds could be. Seemed silly now, but at the time, it had felt like the end of the world. Her heart had been so broken, but then, one day, she'd been over it.

She'd never given it much thought. She'd been a kid, just moving from whim to whim.

Obviously, she'd gotten over it because Finn had cast a peace spell over her. It was rude to magic someone who didn't even know about magic, but also sweet.

Very sweet.

On the next page, he'd doodled a thimbleweed. It was her favorite flower despite it being an invasive weed. There had been a patch in the backyard. On the next page, Finn had apparently experimented with the thimbleweed to see what it could be used for. It was an herbal remedy for coughing.

Apparently, it was also good for love spells.

The last line was dated on her sixteenth birthday. It was a lunar spell for enhancing magic. Unlike the other spells, which had little notations about how the spell went, this one just had a question mark.

Had he cast it, and it not worked?

When she turned the page, there was one last entry. A finding spell. It was so hastily scrawled that she could barely read it, and there were no notes.

After that, the pages were blank. If Helena had bound this for Finn, she obviously meant for him to continue with his magical work. Did he even know this book existed?

She would have to show him. Once she found the courage to face him again. Maybe it would help him resolve whatever feelings he had about Helena. He deserved that.

BECAUSE SHE DIDN'T WANT to return back to the house, she took Sugar with her to the bar and hoped Sage wouldn't kick her out. To her surprise, the bar was closed, and there was a note explaining that the bar would return to regular hours tomorrow.

Pulling out her phone, she called Sage.

"The kitchen door is open," Sage said immediately. "Come on back. Ginger is here."

Kitchen. Hmm. "I have Sugar with me."

"Oh, you brought the demon dog. Okay, don't put him down in the kitchen. We're on the roof. You remember how to get here."

"Demon dog!"

Sage had already hung up. Scowling, Paris went around the back. Per Sage's orders, she didn't put Sugar down. Just like when she was a kid, she headed straight for the stairs by the office and climbed them. There were no dining options on the roof, but Sage's father often banished them up there when they were underfoot.

On the roof, she put Sugar down and glared at Sage. "Demon dog?" She repeated

"That's what everyone in town is calling him. Debbie Pickard said he bit her on the ankles when she was taking out the trash."

"Debbie Pickard kicked at him! Of course, he bit her."

With a laugh, Ginger leaned down and held out a French fry. Sugar snatched it up immediately with a happy grumble, and his thin little tail wagged furiously. "Come sit down and eat."

Sugar didn't seem at all concerned with exploring the edge of the roof while there was food available, so Paris joined them at the small table. Looking around, she grinned. "You've been doing some work up here. Planning on opening up a dining area?"

"I was thinking about it. The problem is that the staircase isn't in a great location or big enough for servers with trays. Building a new one is costly," Sage sighed. "But it would be nice."

"So have a dumbwaiter installed. Several." Paris lifted the bun off her burger. "Turkey burger with strawberry jam. You remembered."

"Hard to forget that. Dumbwaiters are kind of brilliant. I'll have a contractor take a look."

"It was your dad's idea. You kept yelling at him for things down the steps, and he delivered food, drinks, and utensils. I wanted ice cream, so I followed him down one day. I didn't want to ask him to make another trip, and your dad was muttering about getting dumb waiters installed for us," Paris explained.

Sage snorted. "Figures. He grumbled a lot when you two came over, but it was always half-hearted. Ginger, you moved into your mom's house?"

"I did. Sort of feels like nothing has changed. Paris is at Helena's manor. I'm in my mom's house. You're here at the bar." Ginger shook her head. "Except everything has changed. Parents and guardians are gone. I've got a kid. Paris has a demon."

Paris decided to let that slide. "I love Sugar, but I think the kid thing is bigger. How is your daughter settling in?"

"I would love to know that myself, but Ivy is the sullen and quiet type, at least when it comes to me." Ginger laughed dryly. "She's keeping herself entertained, at least."

Paris peered at her old friend and frowned. There were dark circles under her eyes. "You aren't sleeping well."

"No," Ginger admitted. "And it's part of the reason that I asked to have dinner. I've been having nightmares, and I think they might be memories. I'm sorry, Sage. I know you don't want to have anything to do with this —"

"You're right," Sage interrupted. "I didn't want to have

anything to do with this, but I knew you didn't want dinner for old times sake. Tell us about the dreams."

Pursing her lips, Ginger finally took a deep breath and shook her head. "Monsters. It's like the nightmares of children. Horrid, grotesque monsters, and yet, I know they're not real. Not the me dreaming, but the me in the dream. I know they aren't real. I know that the two of you are close, and I know that we're meant to be together. It doesn't make sense."

"Magic," Paris said softly. Sage shot her a look, but Paris didn't regret saying it. Ginger needed to know what they were dealing with. She deserved it. "We were dosed with magic, and our memory was erased by a special type of fae."

"What?" Sage's gaze flew up to hers. "When did you learn that?"

Paris was all set to tell her when she noticed something odd. "You are not surprised," Paris told Ginger with narrow eyes. "You know about magic."

Slowly, Ginger nodded. "I guess we've all been keeping secrets. I don't know much about magic, per se. I know about werewolves. Specifically, when you marry one and reproduce, and then your child is a werewolf, and when that husband leaves you with a ton of questions and no way of helping your child, Silver Mist Cove is apparently the place to go. When I realized that there is magic in the world and magical creatures, It made me realize that magic might have something to do with what happened to us. I've been wanting to bring it up, but I thought it would sound nuts. What do you, the two of you, know?"

"I'm a witch." Paris smiled. A great weight lifted off her shoulders. She hadn't realized how much it burdened her to keep her secret from Ginger. "New witch. I only found out since returning, but apparently, Helena and her coven have been expecting me to come into my powers for a long time."

Ginger's eyes widened. "Helena is a witch. Does that make Finn one, too?"

"If you want to ask about Finn, you should talk to him. I feel strange even telling you that I'm a witch."

Nodding, Ginger turned to Sage. The beauty rolled her eyes and sighed. After a moment, there was a glimmer around her, and Ginger gasped. Sage had dropped her glamour. "Fae, and like I told Paris, I didn't know until I was in my twenties. Being a child in this town is apparently very complicated."

Clearing her throat, Ginger leaned forward and reached for one of Sage's vines. The beauty knocked her hand away and scowled. "No touching."

"So a human, a fae, and a witch get kidnapped, dosed with magic, and memories erased." Ginger leaned back in her chair and wrinkled her nose. "I can't say I expect that I was the target, being the human. Paris didn't have magic then. Sage?"

"When I found out who my father was, I asked him if I was the target. My father was a powerful man, but he said that no one reached out. No one demanded a ransom of any kind. Then, I started having dreams. Monsters. Just like you. I started investigating."

That was news to Paris. Sage had been the one against their investigation. "You did? What did you find?"

"Not much. Just a lot of information that didn't make any sense. When I got frustrated, I put it all away. I tried to put it behind me. I was angry at my father for a long time. I thought he was to blame. That I was to blame for what happened to us."

Paris's throat tightened. Sage thought she was to blame, but Paris suspected that it was her. Something she had done that night. "I lured us out there. I wanted to do something; I just can't remember. I'm pretty sure it's all my fault."

"No," Sage growled. "I learned that even if they were after me, it wasn't my fault, and it's not yours either. Someone did this to us, and you're right. We need to find out what happened. I've got that box of information buried somewhere. I'll have to dig it up. Maybe something in there will help us. In the meantime, why do you think a fae wiped our memories?"

"We have a lot to catch up on."

CHAPTER 22
FINN

elena knew the power of respect, but she would have hated seeing Finn in a suit at her funeral, so he compromised. Dark dress pants but with a green button-up shirt. No jacket and no tie. He rolled his shirt up to his elbows and carried forget-me-nots in his pocket.

The house was somber today. It seemed to know that Helena's funeral was today. Finn waited at the front door. It had been a couple of days since he and Paris had spoken at length. If she wanted to be alone, he would give her the freedom to go to the funeral alone, but he wanted her to know that he was there for her.

If she still wanted him.

When she appeared at the top of the steps, she wore green. The cotton dress was fitted with short sleeves and a scoop neck and stopped just above her knee. She'd swept her blonde hair up into a neat bun, and she wore a silver medallion around her neck.

The tree of life.

"Helena got it for me one birthday," she said when she

reached the foot of the stairs. "It's been a long time since I wore it."

Finn swallowed and nodded. "I remember. She wanted a different necklace. A Celtic knot, and she sent me to the store to get it. I switched it out at the last minute. The tree just seemed more like you. Helena was annoyed, but when she saw it, she knew I made the right decision."

She touched her necklace, and the soft smile she gave him rocked him to his core. "Then I'm sorry I put it away when I was mad at Helena. You look nice."

"So do you." Finn wanted to say more, to tell her that she looked more than nice, but that was a conversation for after the funeral. "I was waiting to see if you wanted a ride. If you want to go alone —"

"I don't. I would love a ride."

It seemed like the beginning of a truce, although Finn didn't know what she was thinking. She'd come back late that night and was gone the next day. In fact, she'd been very busy for the past couple of days.

He'd missed her. He wanted to explain, but nothing had changed. She had a great destiny in front of her. He would only stand in her way.

"It's perfect that you are having her funeral in the gardens. I don't know how you got them to agree to that, but Helena would love it. And it's a beautiful day, although I imagine Helena did something ahead of time to make certain that it would be a perfect day."

"Not everything was in Helena's control." As soon as Finn said the words, a strange sense of calm came over him. "And try as she might, she couldn't see everything."

"Those words will probably bring her back to life," Paris joked as they reached the car. When Finn leaned over to open the door, he put a hand on her waist. She inhaled deeply, and he knew what he would see if he looked at her face.

All that open vulnerability.

"I loved Helena, and I'll miss her, but her time is gone," he said as he opened the door. "The future belongs to us, Paris."

With a smile, she slipped into the car. It was that smile that he'd missed in the last few days. The knot in his chest loosened, and he almost whistled as he walked to the driver's side. Something had changed in him. His path was clearer than ever. It was just a strange day to see it.

Or maybe it was the perfect day.

The Silver Mist Cove Gardens was hardly an event venue. The community gardens had fallen into disarray quite a few years ago until Helena stepped in. Through hard work, and Finn suspected some magic, Helena turned the gardens from tangled weeds into a lush area of raised beds with lettuce, vegetables, fruits, and herbs. If anyone wondered how tropical fruits were thriving so far north, no one said anything.

Since her work, the community had stepped in, and the gardens thrived, even in the winter. It wasn't set up for events, but when Finn asked Duke if they could make it happen, he readily agreed. Memorial flowers were erected, as well as large tents to help shade from the sun. Chairs were set up along the perimeter, and Helena's urn was in the middle. She'd said time and time again that the last thing she wanted was for anyone to have access to her dead body.

Finn had joked that he didn't think anyone had the power to reanimate her from a plucked strand of hair, and Helena had sharply reminded him that he lived in a town of impossible creatures.

"Oh, Finn. This is perfect. She would love it," Paris whispered. "It's the perfect place to say goodbye."

Curious, he looked down at her. "You seemed to have forgiven her."

"Little by little, I'm learning more about Helena now that she's gone than I ever did when she was alive. I don't necessarily know that there's anything to forgive. I'm just trying to remember that she was human, and she made mistakes. Or maybe she had her reasons." Tears filled her eyes. "I'm going to say goodbye before the funeral starts. I imagine the whole town will turn out."

She was right. There were so many people in attendance that people ended up standing well outside the hearing range of the speakers. Finn started, welcoming everyone and thanking them for coming. He was surprised when a lump formed in his throat, but he looked at Paris and gained control. After a few words, he stepped aside. Annie and Duke had promised to do most of the speaking, as well as some of Helena's good friends from the coven. It felt unfair to turn it over to them, but they had volunteered.

When Finn took his seat, he noticed that the two seats next to Paris were taken by Ginger and Sage. They all held hands. It was like no time had passed. Something had happened, and they were bonded just as before.

In fact, the more he looked at Paris, the more he realized that they were bonded even more than before.

There was a magical aura surrounding them. One that hadn't been there before.

THEY HELD the wake at the manor. People moved in and out all afternoon, swapping their favorite Helena stories.

Finn listened absentmindedly. He didn't feel guilty about it. Helena would understand if she could see what he saw.

Why, he wondered, didn't anyone else see it? Whenever Sage, Ginger, and Paris were together, warmth filled the room along with a hazy golden glow. Everyone kept on like nothing strange was happening.

"Finn! There you are! I have been looking all over for you," Marigold said brightly as she hurried his way. "I just put a few dozen cupcakes on the pot-luck table, but I wanted to make sure that you had one personally. I know how hard this can be."

"Marigold," Finn said warily. He hadn't seen much of his neighbor after they all but accused her of stealing the book. Now, she was smiling cheerfully like nothing had happened.

That smile was a little too bright for a funeral wake.

"Thank you." He held the cupcake, but it was clear from Marigold's expression that she wasn't leaving until he tasted it. Dutifully, he peeled the liner and took a bite. "It's great, thank you."

"I am so glad that you like it. I'm thinking of starting my own business. Fill the hole that Helena left behind."

"Aren't there several bakeries in town?" Finn asked in confusion. Helena's baking had been amazing, but she was hardly the only game in town. There wasn't any hole to fill.

Marigold just chuckled and floated away with her tray of cupcakes. Finn took another bite of the cupcake and frowned. It was a familiar taste, but he couldn't quite place it.

"Hey. You good, man?" Zane appeared, a strange look on his face. He held out his hand, and Finn shook it. "Lot of people here."

"Helena was a force. Some people loved her. Most people just respected her. I appreciate you being here."

"Yeah, I..." Zane's voice trailed off, and he frowned. Finn looked over his shoulder. Paris, Sage, and Ginger were together again. Their glow was unmistakable. "I figured I would stop by and see how you were doing."

Could Zane see the glow? "Everything okay?"

"Yeah. Sorry. That's my neighbor. I haven't been over to say hello yet. I guess it would be weird to do it at a funeral."

"Ginger? Probably not."

"She has a daughter." Zane still couldn't seem to take his eyes off Ginger.

"She does. Ivy."

"So there's a husband? Boyfriend?"

"Ex-husband. No longer in the picture." Finn waited for a beat. "See something you like, Zane?"

The werewolf's eyes tinged gold for just a second before they faded. "Nothing like that. Just used to that house being empty." He clapped Finn on the shoulder. "Let me know if you need anything." Then, with a frown, he sniffed the air. "Did you get a dog?"

"Paris. She has a chihuahua. I...ah...convinced her to keep him up in her room for the wake."

Zane grinned. "The demon dog. I've heard about him."

"His name is Sugar."

"Of course it is. I'll be seeing you around, Finn."

The wolf ducked away just before a hand touched Finn's shoulder. He turned to see Paris with a cupcake in her hand and an annoyed look on her face. "Have you eaten one of these?"

He held up his eat cupcake. "Marigold practically threw it in my face."

"And?"

There was obviously something that he wanted from her. "It's good. Not quite as good as Helena's, but still good."

"It doesn't take familiar to you?"

"Sure, but..." he frowned. "My graduation."

"Yeah, High school graduation. Helena made these cupcakes, especially for you. You liked them so much that you told her she should *only* make them for you. She agreed. She never made these for anyone else, but she wrote the recipe down. I tried to remake them once when she was mad at me. I thought it might give me some brownie points if I could recreate them."

Finn could see where Paris was heading. If Helena had written the recipe down, and Marigold was trying to recreate them, that could only mean two things. One that Helena had told her, which he highly doubted. Or two, that Marigold had found the recipes. "Marigold stole Helena's recipe books."

"She did. I wonder what else she did to get her hands on them and what else she might have taken."

CHAPTER 23
FINN

Finn pulled Marigold aside and thanked her again for the cupcakes. When he asked her to stay after and help them clean up, she seemed almost pleased. They were surrounded by people, and her face glowed as she touched his arm and told him that she wanted to do all that she could to help.

Privately, fury boiled beneath his skin, but he held it together until the end of the wake. Ginger left first, followed, Finn noticed, by Zane. Sage left not long after, and Paris busied herself after that, cleaning up plates and glasses. Finn wanted to tell her to stop, but he could see that she needed to keep busy. There were, he noted with displeasure, plenty of people who were giving him their condolences, but not Paris. It was mind-boggling how an entire town could still blame them decades later. They had no proof that the women faked their disappearance, and honestly, in a town full of impossible creatures, how was it that no one could see that something sinister but magical had happened?

No one wants to believe that their neighbors are capable of anything bad.

Helena's voice shook him, and he straightened, waiting for a memory to emerge.

None came. It was as if Helena was standing right next to him and whispering in his ear.

He'd been half joking when he thought that Helena had reached Paris from the grave, but it felt like that was exactly what she was doing to him.

It was not welcome, and he did his best to convey that.

Just as everyone was leaving, Annie walked over and gave him a big hug. "There is just something about being back in this house. It's almost like she's still here with us. Oh, I can see that everything is different. The Manor is trying to please you, but her energy is all around."

"Thank you and Duke again for opening up the gardens. I think it's exactly what Helena would have wanted."

"Indeed." Tears tracked down her face, and she sniffed and wiped them away. "Look at me. I'm just being an old fool. I suppose you're eager to get away from all this chaos and head back home, but it has been nice to see you. I'm sure that Helena was the only reason you came to visit, but I do hope you'll come back. When are you leaving? Have you settled any plans for the house?"

Before he could answer, she sighed and shook her head. "I'm sorry. I'm anxious, and when I'm anxious, I ask a bunch of questions that have nothing to do with me. Promise that you won't sneak out in the middle of the night without saying goodbye."

"I promise."

Duke caught sight of his wife, shook his head, and walked over. He gently pulled her away from Finn and held out his hand. "Helena would have been pleased. You did right by her."

"I was just asking your wife to thank you for all you did."

"No need to thank me. Helena did a lot for this community. Want us to stay and help clean up? I'm sure you and Paris are overwhelmed."

"I asked Marigold, and she graciously agreed," Finn said as he watched a few more people line up to say goodbye. He was getting a little irritated with the people who wanted to say goodbye to him and not Paris. "But thank you for the help."

"Of course."

The crowd thinned more rapidly after Annie and Duke left. There were no somber feelings as the Manor grew more empty. Many of the witches in Helena's coven cast small spells before they left. Blessings. Negative energy banishments. Remembrance spells. The magic lingered, and Manor played with it. When Finn concentrated, he could almost see the sparks of joy in the air.

Finally, he, Paris, and Marigold were the last ones. Paris, attempting to keep busy, had cleared out most of the dirty dishes, and Marigold was helping to load the dishwasher. Once it was full, she closed it and straightened. "I'm sure you two want to be alone with your thoughts. Today was an overwhelming and emotional day. If you need anything, please let me know."

Typical. Marigold wanted to stick around and help until there was no one left to see her hard work. Finn moved quickly to block her from leaving the kitchen, and Paris straightened. "There is one other thing I wanted to discuss with you."

"Oh? What is that?"

"The recipe for those cupcakes that you brought over."

Her eyes lit up with delight. "They were amazing, weren't they? I can't give out my recipes, you know."

"They were okay," Paris said flatly from behind. "They were so much better when Helena made them. There is just something about her baking that I don't think anyone can copy, even after they steal the recipe."

"Excuse me?" Fury flashed in her face, and she turned and rounded on Paris. The happy-go-lucky, innocent, happy-to-help neighbor was gone. "What exactly are you insinuating?"

Paris was clearly fired up, and she wasn't going easy on her. "I'm not insinuating anything. I'm point-blank saying it. You made a mistake when you chose the recipe that you did. It was a special one, made just for Finn. I know Helena never made it for anyone else. Her baking supplies are gone, as well as her recipe books and her spell books. You took them, and I can't help but wonder if that theft has anything to do with the dead body we found in the Manor."

"What?!" Marigold shrieked. "How dare you! How would you know what Helena did and didn't do? You were gone for decades, and good riddance!"

The house rumbled, and Marigold gasped and reached out to steady herself. As soon as her hand touched the counter, it turned bright red. With a shriek, she snatched her hand away. "What is happening?"

"The manor is upset because you keep lying to us," Paris said calmly. "I wouldn't be surprised if it tries to trap you here until you tell the truth."

"Ridiculous. As if there's enough power left for the Manor to even do that. It fed off Helena. You and Finn are nothing," Marigold snapped. "Move out of my way."

Finn moved, but the door behind him slammed shut.

The older woman stumbled back. "You're doing this, some-how. I demand that you stop it."

"I'm not doing anything. Nocturnal nature magic, remember?" Finn said calmly. "And Paris, well, she's still getting to know her magic. Helena was quite the witch, wasn't she? This house has been alive for as long as I can remember. One time, it filled my room with bees for three whole hours. It was pretty upset about the hole I acciden-tally knocked into the wall."

"Bees!" Marigold shook her head. "No...I.... don't believe you."

The kitchen window opened just a crack, and she raced over and attempted to pry it open the rest of the way. When buzzing noises filled the room, she shrieked and backed away. "All right. All right, I took the damn recipe books. And the baking equipment and ingredients. Are you happy? But I didn't kill anyone. I was hauling out the last of everything when I heard the front door open."

The window slammed shut, and the buzzing stopped. Finn couldn't believe it. He hadn't actually thought that Marigold was capable of murder, but was she really there the night Darren broke in?

"What did you do?" He demanded.

"I snuck into the laundry room." Marigold's shoulders deflated. "I could hear Darren. He was trying to set up a spell of some sort. I could hear him incanting some kind of ward, but it didn't seem to be something that was meant to keep people out. He left, and I hurried out the back. That's it. I didn't see him come back. I didn't see anyone else. I didn't know anything bad was going to happen to him."

"A ward?" Paris looked at Finn. "Did you feel a ward when you entered the house?"

He shook his head. "No. The only magic was the manors."

"Do you remember what he said?"

Marigold pursed her lips together, and when he took a step forward, she wrinkled her nose. "All right, all right. Fine. I started recording in the middle. I didn't even know Darren had magic, and I wanted a record of it. It wasn't in English, and I couldn't make anything out. Here. I'll send it to you."

Pulling out her phone, she fumbled with it and stopped. "I'll send it to you if you promise not to go to the cops."

"A man is dead, Marigold, and you were a witness. Don't you want to help?" Paris asked softly.

"Then I would have to explain what I was doing here, wouldn't I? Helena struggled to keep up with her business as she got older. I offered to help. I told her we could be partners, but she refused. She was rude about it, too. I figured it wasn't going to hurt anyone to take her recipes."

"And her spell books?"

The witch whirled around on Paris. "I didn't take any spell books! The basement was magically locked, anyway. Couldn't even if I wanted to."

The...basement?

Paris gasped and met Finn's gaze. He knew what she was thinking. The basement. How could they have forgotten that the Manor had a basement? The door was right off the kitchen. They saw it every day, several times a day, and yet he hadn't paid any attention to it.

Turning his head, he stared. There it was. A regular door. Sitting there like it must have been this whole time but somehow hidden from them.

Helena. Just what kind of game was she playing?

"Send us the recording, Marigold," Paris said softly.

"And return the recipe books. They're special to Finn. We won't tell the sheriff."

Marigold clutched her phone. "Can I copy the recipes?"

"Marigold, don't you want to stand apart from Helena? To make a name for yourself that's separate from hers? You don't want to be the woman who made Helena's cupcakes after she died. You want to be known for your own recipes. Your cupcakes were good. You can come up with your own recipes," Paris said gently.

Nodding, the woman muttered to herself. A few minutes later, Finn's phone vibrated. He checked it to make sure that it was the audio file.

"Now, can I go," she asked, glaring at the ceiling.

The door opened, and she muttered something about the magical house being a real pain in her neck. Paris stared at Finn. "You should go with her to collect the books."

"Fine, but you stay here. We'll go to the basement together. I don't know what she did to it, and I don't want you to get hurt."

Paris nodded. "I'll be right here waiting."

CHAPTER 24
PARIS

Paris waited for Finn to get back before she attempted to open the door, but while she waited, she sat cross-legged in front of it and stared.

Really stared.

How could she have forgotten a whole section of the house? How could she have walked by this door over and over again and not seen it?

And how, knowing what she knew right now, could she not see the magic surrounding it? It had to be some powerful glamour to hide not just from sight but from their memories.

"The spell can't just dissipate like that. I should be able to see it. Did you do this?" She demanded of the Manor. "Have you been deliberately keeping Finn and me out?"

The house didn't respond, but she could feel its hurt. Sighing, she placed her hand on the floor. "I'm sorry. I know. You're here to help."

If it wasn't the house, then it was Helena. Why would she want to keep Paris out of the basement?

Annabelle thought she'd had magic for years. She could

see it in her aura. What if Helena had done something to her to make her forget her magic? To make her not be able to feel it?

A new fear blossomed inside of her. What if Helena thought Paris couldn't handle her magic? What if closing off the basement had been to protect her?

Every time she thought she could forgive Helena of something, something else cropped up. Something else that Helena had done that was hurtful.

"Paris? What are you doing?" A loud thud broke her attention, and she turned as Finn dropped a stack of books and hurried to her. "Did you fall?"

"No. I just sat here. I was waiting. I thought...I wanted to try and see the spell veiling the basement door. I can see magic. I should be able to see it. Plus, I was a little worried that I would turn my head, and it would be gone again."

"I don't think that's going to happen." Holding out his hand, he helped her up. "Needing to get back to you, and the basement was the only thing that kept me from strangling Marigold."

Get back to you.

Paris's heart did somersaults, but she tried not to let it show. It's not what Finn meant, and she wasn't going to let the turmoil of everything else happening to feed false hope. They were meant to be friends. Good friends and she was going to have to be okay with that. It was good. Right then, she didn't think she would be able to go on if Finn wasn't there for her in some capacity.

Finn continued. "I can't see the spell either, which tells me that Aunt Helena cast it. She could hide her magic, a very rare talent. I just don't understand why she did it."

"To keep me out of it," Paris said flatly.

"Are you kidding? All she wanted was for you to wield

your magic. There has to be a different reason. I bet she's got dead bodies in there."

Paris was thankful for his small attempt at humor, but she couldn't even summon the smallest of smiles. "Are you ready to open it?"

Holding her breath, she nodded. Time seemed to slow as he reached out and turned the doorknob.

Nothing happened.

Frowning, he jiggled it. Then, with a grumble under his breath, he fit both hands around the door and pulled.

"She magically sealed it," he said, disbelief in his voice. "She not only hid it, but she magically sealed it. Are you kidding me?"

Hysteria bubbled up inside her, but she pushed it down. "How do you magically seal something?"

"Generally with a blood ward, but I'm her blood. The fact that she didn't use it means she was sealing it against me. What on earth could be down there that she needs to be hidden so badly?" Stepping back, he stared at the door thoughtfully. "Maybe she only sealed it against me. You try opening it."

"Okay. Should I try to use magic or..."

"No. Just think of it as a regular door. No magic.."

Feeling foolish, Paris touched the door knob. She half expected to feel a shock or a jolt, but it wasn't even warm. When she turned it, there was no movement. With a grunt, she pulled. "Nothing. So now what?"

"So now we leave it. I need to do some research on magically releasing the spell, and unfortunately, there aren't any spellbooks left. Maybe someone in her coven, or Marigold's cove now, can help. I have a feeling it's going to take a good amount of power, and we're already emotion-ally drained." Paris couldn't help herself. She started flipping through the one spell book they had. There were a number of spells to break seals. Some of them included a paste to put over the seal and words to melt the seal away. Others included what essentially seemed like a magical bomb to break the seal.

There were a number of spells that simply required her inner magic. Sitting in front of the door cross-legged, she placed her hands on either door side of the door and murmured the incantation.

A shimmer passed through her, and her hope blossomed. Closing her eyes, she repeated the incantation and mentally tried to blast her magic at it.

Nothing. Not even a shimmer.

Frustrated, she pushed the book aside and flipped through another one until she found what she was looking for. It was for opening magical doorways, and while that wasn't exactly what she was looking for, she figured she'd give it a shot.

Replacing her hands, she started to mutter the words.

"Paris," Finn shouted. "No."

Abruptly, she pulled her hands away. "What?"

"Let's not open portals to other worlds."

"Portals to...oh." Embarrassed, she closed the book. "It hadn't occurred to me that you could even do that."

"Magic can do all kinds of things. You're taxing yourself out. Take a break."

Frustrated, she stood and all but kicked a book. "She did this on purpose. She knew I had my magic, and she, for whatever reason, hid it from me. Maybe she thinks I won't be any good at it, or maybe she thinks I don't deserve it. Now, my answers are probably just beyond that door, and I'm not a good enough witch to get to them! Is it a test? Is she just punishing me?"

"If all that's true, then I'm also not a good enough witch to open it," Finn pointed out.

"She probably did something so that your magic specifically can't open it. She knows your magic."

Finn snorted. "Actually, she doesn't. Helena never bothered to learn my magic. I wasn't powerful enough to interest her. Not like she expected you to be or like you are."

Ignoring that last part, Paris walked away to her bag. "You're wrong. She knows your magic very well. Unless you made a book of all your spells." Returning, she thrust the book his way. "I looked through it. You were writing spells when you were a child. Spells that worked."

A look of astonishment crossed his face as he reached out and took the book. Without a word, he sat down at the table and started to flip through it.

He needed to be alone, and maybe she did too. "I'm going to take a walk to clear my head. I don't know how long I'll be. A bunch of people shoved some casseroles in the freezer. You should heat one up if you get hungry. I can just reheat the leftovers when I get back.," she said quietly.

"Paris, wait." He jerked his head up and studied her. "Do you want to talk?"

Talk about what? How was Helena still keeping secrets from her? "No. I really don't."

He didn't stop her as she left. Despite saying she needed to take a walk, she didn't want to walk here on the edge of the bluffs. On one side was Marigold and her lies, and on the other were houses full of witches who were waiting for her to take over the coven. She needed to get away. If she wasn't so desperate for answers about her past, she'd leave town entirely.

Instead, she drove to Main Street. It was late enough

that most everything had closed except for a handful of bars and restaurants. Green Brews would be open. She desperately wanted to talk to Ginger and Sage. They could help her sort through her thoughts and feelings. At least, they used to.

Now, so much time has passed, and they have their own lives to worry about. Sage was trying to get away from magic. Ginger had a werewolf daughter to worry about. They weren't teenagers anymore. No matter how much she wished they could be there for her, it wasn't fair to ask them.

Sitting on one of the benches, she stared up at the night sky. She'd thought she'd just lost three days. Instead, she'd lost a whole piece of herself for decades, and now, she wasn't sure how to put it all back together.

Her phone buzzed. Pulling it out, she stared at it. "Sage?" The greeting was a question when she answered.

"Are you all right?" Sage demanded.

What? How could Sage possibly know that she was in need of her friends? "I'm fine. Why?"

"Because I have this strange feeling that you need me. Where are you? I've already closed up the bar early. I found the box I was looking for."

"I'm actually just a block from you," Paris said slowly. "But I don't need..."

"Can you come by?"

"I can."

"Good. Oh, that's Ginger calling me. Maybe she can swing by, too. I'll open a bottle of wine and get some chips and queso dip going."

Paris couldn't help but smile. "That sounds great."

CHAPTER 25

PARIS

As soon as Paris entered the bar, Sage jumped up and hugged her. "Are you all right?"

"I'm fine. Honestly." Paris wanted to collapse in her friend's arms. There was something so warm and comforting about them. It was the first real hug they'd shared since she got back. "If I was sending out some strange witchy signals, I didn't mean to. Is Ginger coming? I'm so embarrassed. It's late. I hope she's not leaving her daughter—"

"Stop that," Sage said firmly. "Stop that right now. We're your friends, and if you need us, then we're here for you. Full stop. End of story. Today has been such a long day for you."

That much was true. It almost felt like Helena's funeral was a month ago instead of this morning. "I guess if Ginger is coming, I'll wait until she gets here to tell you the whole story. It doesn't have anything to do with our disappearance, or maybe it does. It's so frustrating trying to untangle all the threads."

"And figure out who is lying and who isn't?" Sage said darkly. "I know."

Paris stared at her friend, and her heart sank. "You found the box, didn't you?"

"I did, and I think I know why I'd given up to begin with. Like you said, though, we should wait for Ginger. She should be here any minute."

Sage picked up a bar rag, and Paris eyed it with interest. "Can I help? I'd love to do something a little more active rather than just standing here and waiting."

"Want to sweep?"

"I would love to sweep."

For fifteen minutes, Paris got lost in the rhythmic strokes of the broom. The simple forward and back motion was comfortable, and the only thing that kept her from completely withdrawing was the fact that she had to pile up the trash for the dustbin. Still, her mind wandered.

And her anger intensified. How dare Marigold? First the coven and then the baking? Was she trying to steal Helena's life? And Helena! Did she think she was trying to protect Paris? It was one thing to protect a scared and confused teenager, but Paris was neither. She didn't need protection. If anything, Helena's protection was putting her in a precarious position. She was surrounded by magic and knew so little of her own. What if someone did try and attack her? Then what?

"Paris? Paris, I think you can stop now. You're drenching my bar in magic."

Sage's panicked voice cut through Paris's anger, and she stopped. Looking up, she watched, in fascination, as her magic swirled around her. She didn't need to analyze it to know what it was doing.

It was protecting her.

"Sorry. I was angry at Helena and Marigold, and I just got lost in my own thoughts. I guess when I'm really upset, I start leaking magic, and the sweeping intensified it."

"No, it's fine." Sage watched, wide-eyed, as the dust settled. "Is this protection magic?"

"I think so. I read that sweeping can do that. Sweep away negative energy and form a barrier of protection. I can try to dispel it."

"What, and let the evil just walk in? No, thank you. This will do just fine. I'll pay you in free drinks," Sage said with a grin on her face. "You know, in a place like Silver Mist Cove, you feel a lot of magic, but there's something about your magic. It suits me."

"It suits you?" Paris repeated with a grin.

"It feels nice."

"Do you and my magic need to be alone together?" She teased.

Sage snorted. "It doesn't feel that nice, although if you could conjure me a man who's quiet, knows everything I like, and only exists between sundown and sunup, I wouldn't say no."

"Wouldn't that be grand?"

"Really? I found it difficult that you'd be interested in that kind of thing, especially with Finn living in the house?" Sage waved her hand. "No, don't answer that. Ginger is here, and she's going to ask you the very same question."

Sure enough, less than thirty seconds later, Ginger appeared at the door. Sage unlocked it and quickly locked it behind her. Still in her pajamas with her red hair still tousled in a messy bun on top of her head, Ginger looked like she'd just rolled out of bed. "Something is different in here."

"It's Paris's magic," Sage said with a grin. "Feels good, right?"

"It feels great!"

Chuckling, Paris rolled her eyes. "All right, if the two of you plotted behind my back to try and do something to make me feel better about my magic, you can stop. It's weird when you say my magic feels good."

"I'm just telling you what I feel." Ginger's eyes scanned the bar. "Please tell me there is wine."

"There is wine," Sage obliged her.

"Ginger, did you get out of bed? I feel terrible."

"Oh, this? No, this was what I put on as soon as I left Helena's funeral. It just felt like a pajama and messy-bun kind of night. Then I felt your frustration, which was weird. And Sage's fury, which was equally weird. What is going on with you two? And why am I feeling it? Mundane human over here."

That was strange. "Sage, you were upset? I didn't feel anything."

"Your frustration and...I don't even know how to explain it. Self-doubt? It was overwhelming. I'm not surprised you couldn't feel anything else," Ginger said kindly. "Right after we talk about why both of you were feeling that way, then we can figure out why we're feeling each other's emotions?"

They both looked at her expectantly, and Paris raised her hands. "I didn't cast a spell for anything like that. I swear."

Sage sighed. "No, we want you to tell us what's going on."

"Oh. Right." Quickly, she filled them in on Marigold, what she saw, and the door. "I swear I think Helena is responsible for why I've gone so long without knowing I have magic. I just can't figure out why. Or what's changed? I have magic now. Why can't I open the door?"

"It might have something to do with this." Walking around behind the bar, Sage pulled out a box. "After everything happened, and when the town turned on us, I felt so lost. When you two left, I missed you. I wanted to leave as well, and I felt so alone. My father told me to drop it, but I couldn't. I needed to do something with my anger and fear. I started digging. I broke into the sheriff's station for the file. I tried to wrangle some information out of a young FBI agent. I learned about my heritage a few months later. My father had power. Real power and I tried to tap into whatever I had to use. That's when my father stepped in and told me, under no uncertain terms, to let it go. Let it go, or else."

Paris grabbed the bottle of wine and poured them three hefty glasses. At the same time, Sage grabbed the platter of wine and crackers. Instead of sitting at the table like adults, they did what they used to. Sat cross-legged in front of the gas fireplace. Sage brought the box over.

"Or else what?" Ginger asked softly. "He couldn't possibly threaten you. He had to know something."

"At the time, I dropped it. Or so I thought. I was a dutiful daughter. My father asked me to stop, and I did, but I was angry. I'm still angry. Especially now."

Paris didn't understand. "You found something in the box?"

"That's just it. I hadn't thought about this box in years. I thought about the missing nights. The nightmares. But not about what I'd looked into. Not about what I learned. Not until the two of you came back. Then, it was like slowly wiping away the dust and dirt and discovering a memory. I'm still trying to clear the cobwebs."

Opening the box, she pulled out some folders. "I stole

the original file from the sheriff's office. You can look through it, but there's not much there. This," she said, pulling out a thick book," is the journal I kept. I talked to witnesses. I wrote down my nightmares. I tried to make sense of them. Then, there's this."

Paris and Ginger leaned forward as Sage opened the journal and flipped through it. "I remember the day I stopped investigating. September tenth. The date is seared into my brain, but look at this." She pointed to the date at the top of the entry.

"September eleventh," Paris read. "You kept investigating after you thought you stopped. You think your memory is faulty?"

"No. I think my memory was altered," Sage growled. "This journal goes through two additional months of investigation, including Samhain and Thanksgiving. I would remember that. Furthermore, my investigation shifted."

"To?" Ginger asked anxiously.

"To my father and Helena." Sage's eyes met Ginger's. "And your mother."

"What? What are you talking about?" Ginger grabbed the journal and whipped it around. "Sage, I can't read your chicken scratch. What is this?"

"They started meeting in the bar every night. At first, I thought that maybe they were trying to figure out what happened to us. Your mother and Helena were upset that you two were gone, but they kept saying that it was good that you had left town. It was for the best. I didn't understand why they would say such a thing, so I started trying to record what they said."

Paris's heart sped up just a little. Fear crept in. She had doubts about Helena. Paranoia that Helena had something to do with this, but despite everything, she'd desperately wanted to be wrong. Helena loved her. She wouldn't do anything to hurt her.

But was Sage about to show her evidence of the contrary?

"Say it fast," Paris whispered. "Just rip off the bandaid."

Reaching over, Sage took her hand and squeezed it. "I wish it was something simple like that. I could just come out and say that they all knew who had kidnapped us, but they didn't. They were looking into it, but they seemed to know what happened to us. They just never came right out and said it. They talk a lot about a bond."

"A bond? Our bond? Like our friendship?" Ginger asked.

"I don't think so. My father and your mother kept saying that the bond was never meant to happen. That it wasn't destined for us. Helena believed that it was meant to be; it just wasn't meant to happen then. She said the whole town would feel its effects."

Wrinkling her nose, Ginger leaned back and smirked. "We caused some trouble, but I don't think the whole town felt the effects of us leaving. Obviously, it's some other kind of bond."

"In the last entry, I wrote that my father knew I was following him. I don't remember writing this. That I don't remember writing any of this is my father's handiwork." Sage spun the box around and pointed to a small symbol in the corner. "This is my father's symbol. It's centuries old."

"Centuries," Ginger squeaked. "Sage, are you going to live that long?"

"Trust me, that is not something that I want to think about. Anyway, I didn't doodle this. I've tried to recreate it ever since I learned about it. There's no way I drew it this perfectly and forgot about it. This is my father's handiwork."

Paris stared at it. It seemed to move before her very eyes. Serpentine over itself. "I can see the power there. What does it mean?"

"It's a little hard to explain. When he marks something with this, he can take ownership of it and manipulate anything attached to it. He took ownership of my information and then, somehow, manipulated my memories."

"But then he didn't get rid of it."

"Part of the spell. Let's say he burned the journal. It's no longer in the box, and his symbol is no longer attached to it. Thus, he no longer has control over it. I would remember it. Instead, he takes away my will to keep investigating. To even look in the box again." Tears filled her eyes. "I just don't understand why he would do something like that."

Ginger opened her mouth and before she whipped her head around. "Do you smell that?"

Paris sniffed. "From the fire?"

"Not this fire." Ginger slowly stood. "But that is definitely smoke from a fire."

Paris and Sage rose at the same time. The air shimmered around them. "That... that's my protection spell. Can you feel that?"

Sage shuddered. "It feels like something is trying to hammer their way into the bar."

She walked to the window and opened the blinds. Everyone screamed at once.

A wall of fire blazed outside the window. Paris raced to the door and put her hand on the doorknob.

It was so hot it scorched her hand, and she snatched it back. "Back exit. Now. We need to get out of here."

They raced to the back, but they couldn't get through

the kitchen. A wall of fire slowly burned through, keeping them from the exit. It was impossible. How could it have gotten so big without them knowing?

"Fire does not move this way," Sage hissed as she grabbed her phone.

"I think it's my protection spell. It's trying to keep the fire at bay, but it's being eaten away." Her heart was lodged in her throat. They were in trouble. Real trouble.

Again.

"My phone isn't working," Sage said in a panic. "Yours?"

Ginger and Paris both tried there. None of them would even turn on.

Pressing together, they linked hands. "I'm not very good at controlling my magic," Paris whispered. "But I'll try my best."

They were trapped. If she couldn't find a way to put the fire out, they were going to burn to death.

"You do that," Sage said gravely. "In the meantime, Ginger? I've got a whole bunch of fire extinguishers."

CHAPTER 26
FINN

He'd been through the book three times, but still, he sat at the table and flipped through it again. The lasagna had burned. He'd only stopped long enough to take the lasagna out after he started to smell it and returned to the table.

When he was a kid, writing down the spells was the only way he could formulate them. It was the only way he could organize his thoughts and make sure he got everything just right.

Later, when he was older, his thoughts would still get jumbled up, but when it came to magic, they were sharper. He rarely wrote things down, but when it came to Paris, it was a compulsion. He had to know that he wasn't going to do anything to hurt her. He had to write things down.

Helena had found them.

He'd crammed his spellwork in the drawer of his desk in his room. Just loose-leaf paper all shoved in there. Some of them crumpled and balled up. She'd taken them, smoothed them out, and bound them.

The blank pages in the back were telling. Helena would

only have added them if she meant for him to use them. To create more spells. She did nothing without a reason.

Staring at the last page, his heart hammered in his chest. Invisible words shimmered on the page. It was a game that Helena used to play with him. Every morning, there would be a blank page waiting for him. Once he found the right spell, the words appeared. Sometimes, it was his to-do list. Most of the time, it was a new spell for him to try.

Helena had left him a message. He hadn't tried to break the spell just yet. He was too afraid of what it would say.

The book was a journey in his past. His magical past but also his feelings for Paris. It had felt so intense then, but then, young love always felt intense. It was easy for him to brush it aside to say that it was just a teenage crush.

This was evidence of the contrary. All the things he'd done for Paris, none of it was for his benefit. It was all for her. Once, he'd tucked a flower in her hair, an enchantment to give her the confidence to ask out the boy she'd been crushing. All he'd ever wanted was to see her happy.

As a kid, he'd shared his work with Helena, but afterward, he realized that his magic was private. Especially the magic involving Paris.

How had she found them? It wasn't like her to go snooping. And what on Earth had possessed her to bind them?

She knew how he felt about Paris. Many of these spells were written long after she'd told him that Paris was destined for more than him. She had to know that he'd never stopped loving Paris.

If he wanted to know how she was feeling when she bound this book, all he had to do was break the spell veiling her letter.

It wouldn't be hard. By now, he knew her magic.

Or at least, he thought he did. That door was something altogether new.

We're going to die.

Finn's head shot up. What was that?

I can't stop it.

Paris.

It was a strange sensation, not like when Helena spoke in his head. She wasn't talking to him. It was a feeling, intense emotions, and they were forming words in his head.

Something was wrong. She was in trouble.

Snatching up his phone, he tried to call her, but it didn't go through. Not even the first ring.

Grabbing his keys, he raced out of the house. He had no idea where she was. Her car was gone. She could be anywhere, but he didn't hesitate. He drove straight to town.

There was no way of explaining how he knew. Every turn he made was instinctive. He didn't know where Paris was, but his magic led him straight to her.

In a bar of flames.

"Finn! Where are you going in such a hurry?" Timothy Darat ambled by Sage's bar. He didn't even blink at the flames shooting out. "That's a terrible parking job."

"What are you talking about?! Has something called the fire department?"

"Fire department? Is there a fire?"

Finn was about to shout at him again when he saw one of the stray cats strolling by. It also didn't seem concerned about the flames.

Magic. Whether the fire was magic or simply veiled

magic, Finn didn't know, but Paris was trapped inside. He could feel her panic.

Paris, I'm here.

Immediately, her panic subsided. She could feel him, just as he could feel her. Another new sensation, but one he couldn't take the time to analyze. He needed to help her.

His magic was best over the Earth, but he had some control over the natural elements. The fact that he couldn't reach these flames told him that it wasn't a natural fire.

Lifting his chin, he let the moon's light wash over him. He couldn't stop it, but Paris could. She was designed for this kind of chaos. He couldn't talk to her. Just feel her and her panicked thoughts.

There was something else he could do.

With the blessing of the moon, he fed Paris magic. Funneled it to her through all the love he had for her.

Finn?

He pushed more magic to her. Instinct would take over. She would take his magic and know exactly what to do.

I'm here, Paris. Douse this fire and come to me.

Finn!

The Earth trembled. The ley line pulsed beneath him, and then the fire began to die.

Not die. Drain into the Earth.

Astonished, Finn watched as the ground smoked. A minute later, a single scorch mark was all that was left. The door opened, and three women burst out.

"Finn! You are here! I could feel you!" Paris launched herself into his arms, and he captured her easily.

Her eyes were wild. "I could feel. All of you. And...your magic. What did you do?"

"What I've always done, Paris. What I'll always do."

Cupping her chin, he stared down at her. "Give you whatever you need."

Covering her mouth with his, he kissed her.

Paris was still tingling.

The fire had done zero damage to the bar, but any living thing it touched had died instantly. Luckily, the only thing living it reached was plant life. If it had reached them, they would have been dead.

Trapped in that building, knowing that there was no way out, Paris had been filled with fear. The kind of fear that should have clung to her for the rest of her life, but with one kiss, Finn had swept it all away.

The feeling of his magic mingling with hers had been incredible. When she wielded her magic, it felt like chaos. Uncontrollable raw power, but Finn's magic was the complete opposite. Strength. Patience. It was how she felt whenever he was near.

Then, she knew what to do. It wasn't a spell. Words hadn't appeared in her head or ingredients for a spell. Finn's magic wound around hers, and she simply felt what she needed to do.

The magic fire needed a magical smothering. Using Finn's magic, she asked the Earth for help. She asked it to open and take the fire in.

The feeling was incredible.

But it was not the reason that her body still tingled the way it did. That hadn't come from power.

That kiss.

Oh, that kiss had been *everything*.

He'd insisted on driving her and Ginger home. Sage was more pissed than shaken, and Paris and Ginger shared her sentiments. Someone had obviously tried to kill them, but this time, they weren't scared kids. After dropping Ginger off and making arrangements to help her pick up her car in the morning, Finn and Paris drove back in silence. It wasn't a long drive, thank goodness, because all Paris wanted to do was kiss him again.

After parking, he took her hand, and they walked to the house together. Only after the front door closed behind him did he draw her into his arms again. "Are you certain that you're okay?"

"I am, thanks to you." She put her hands on his chest and stared up at him. "How did you know where we were? Or that I was even in trouble?"

"I honestly don't know. I could feel your panic." Taking her hands, he kissed them. "I've been fighting how I feel about you for so long. When Helena realized that I was falling in love with you, she told me that you were meant for more things. That you had this big magical destiny ahead of you, and I would only stand in your way. That was the last thing that I wanted to do, so when you started to experience your magic, and you confessed your feelings to me, I thought I was doing exactly what Helena feared."

"Stand in my way? Finn, I'd be dead if you weren't there for me. I wouldn't be able to do any of this without you."

"I should never have let Helena get in my head. This book she made of my spells, I think, was her way of telling me that she was wrong. Of asking me for forgiveness. Why the woman couldn't just come out and say the words, I have no idea. She left a message, but I haven't revealed it yet."

"Do you want to?"

"First, I wanted to tell you that I loved you. That I've always loved you and that no matter what that message says, I will always love you. I'll be here by your side, no matter what is in front of you, if you want me to be."

"Yes!" Wrapping her hands around his neck, she lifted herself up and kissed him again. "Having my magic feels like I'm finally making myself whole again, but you are also another piece. I love you too, Finn."

They took a moment, just holding each other, before Paris broke away. "You want to see what Helena wrote now or in the morning?"

"Might as well do it now." He kissed the top of her head. "Are you up for it?"

"I couldn't go to sleep right now even if I tried," she admitted. Her heart was still racing.

Holding hands, they walked to the kitchen, where Finn had left the notebook wide open. She followed him to the kitchen drawer, where he pulled out a needle. Fascinated, she watched as he pricked his finger, and blood welled up. Touching the page, he whispered, "*Blood to blood, reveal. Be hidden no more.*"

It was a blood spell. More specifically, Helena's blood.

"She used to hide messages when I was a kid. The blood spell took me the longest to learn to unlock, and it was the most frustrating because it was the simplest. I could feel what the spell wanted from me, but I'd only ever worked with nature magic. Blood magic is not my favorite."

Words appeared on the page. It wasn't a long letter, like Paris had expected, but two sentences.

She is the one for you. When she is ready, and you are with her, the path will be clear, and she will finally be out of the darkness.

"Huh. I didn't expect her to say that she was wrong, but an apology wouldn't hurt," Paris grunted. She was still mad.

Finn chuckled and took her hand. "Come on. I think I know what Aunt Helena meant." He pulled her to the base-ment door.

"You figured out a way to open it?"

"Yes. Together." He brushed his lips across her knuckles and turned the doorknob.

The air shimmered around them, and the door opened.

CHAPTER 27

PARIS

"I took the spell book out that night."

Sage, Ginger, and Paris all stood at the bar early the next morning. It looked like none of them had gotten any sleep. When Paris and Finn unlocked the basement and saw what was inside, it didn't take long to piece together what Helena had done. Paris had texted her friends, who agreed to meet at Sage's the next morning.

"You remember that?"

"I do. As soon as I saw the spell book, I remembered."

The basement that Paris had remembered from her childhood was dusty and filled with junk. She rarely went down there because she'd always found it creepy. Now, she suspected that Helena had glamoured it somehow.

With her eyes open, she could see the space for what it really was: Helena's crafting room. Finn had said that she worked in the attic, but it was nothing compared to what they found in the basement. At some point, she'd moved everything. There were jars and jars of spell work ingredients, journals filled with scrying and tarot notations, spell notes, and personal entries. When Paris had asked Finn if it was the same as he remembered, he told her that it had been glamoured for him as well. He always performed spells in his room or hers.

When she touched Helena's grimoire, a memory had slammed into her. A lightbulb had gone out in her room, and she'd gone into the basement to see if there was a spare. She hadn't seen any of the ritual items, but the book had been on the table, and it had practically sung to her.

She'd opened it up to a specific page and knew she had to do the spell.

"It was a bonding spell," Paris explained.

Sage's eyes widened. "Yes. I remember. You wanted us to do the bonding spell so we could be friends forever. Wow, did that backfire!"

"Did you remember anything else?" Ginger asked.

"No. Finn is still going through Helena's journals, but a lot of time has passed since we went missing. We're not sure what she pieced together or how long it took. He did figure out what Darren was trying to do, which was to trigger my memory remotely. He was using the house like a trap. As soon as I stepped in, what he'd done all those years ago would have reversed, and I would know."

Ginger frowned. "But why? If you remember what had happened, then you would remember what he'd done. Why didn't he just tell you?"

"I don't know. Maybe he was planning on running. I'd asked Anthony if he could reverse it, but he said only Darren could return the memories. Or it could be done with a spell."

"You have a spell?"

"Helena bookmarked it," Paris said with a little laugh. "It's actually the last spell in the book. I think she created it just for us. We have to perform it where the memory was lost."

"I don't suppose she mentioned where we were when we lost the memory, did she?" Sage asked sourly. "Because I don't remember."

"Of course not. That would be too easy." She hesitated because this next part sounded insane. "Finn has made us each some magical sachets to help us open up our intuition."

As she handed them out, Sage took hers and immediately stuffed it in her pockets. Ginger, meanwhile, studied it warily. "This is going to help us?"

"Your daughter can turn into a wolf, but this you're having trouble with?" Sage asked with a small grin.

"Excellent point." Ginger shook her head. "All right. I'm in. Are we doing this now?"

"I think we need to all be absolutely sure that this is what we want," Paris said quietly. "Whatever happened to us is beyond just erasing our memories. Maybe we saw something we shouldn't, and we're putting our lives in even more danger. Or maybe we did something horrible, or something horrible was done to us. We can wait until Finn goes through the journals and try to get more information."

"There is no way that we did something horrible," Ginger said flatly. "Not while we were together and not while we're separate. It's just not who we are. And whatever it was that we saw or did or was done to us, we are strong enough to handle it. No offense to Helena, but I don't know if we can trust her or our parents. I say we do it, and I say we do it now."

Paris looked at Sage and saw her hesitation. "Sage? Please don't try to keep anything in. If you have any reservations, now is the time to voice it."

"No hesitation. I just...whatever we find, I know it's going to be big. It's going to change our future and how we think of ourselves. Ginger, you have a daughter. This could affect her. Paris, you're starting a new relationship. This could change that. Not to mention..." she took a deep breath. "Not to mention that you two could leave again."

Immediately, Paris and Ginger wrapped themselves around Sage in a big hug. They stayed until she groaned and pushed them away. "All right. I get it. We're in this together."

"What's happening is already affecting my daughter," Ginger said firmly. "I don't know what the future holds. Her safety is my primary concern, so if this opens a bigger can of worms and I have to leave to protect her, then I will. But if we're safe, then I'm staying. I have this strange feeling that this is where I'm supposed to be."

Paris couldn't speak for Finn. They spent the night exploring magic rather than talking about their future. Starkly, she realized that while she didn't have any roots, he did. Maybe he didn't want to stay in Silver Mist Cove.

"I can't think of anything that we could find that would break Finn and me apart," she said firmly. "I'm the same with Ginger. I feel like this is where I need to be."

Sage nodded. "Then let's do this. Where should we start? We know where we came out."

"We also know where we would have gone in," Ginger said slowly. "Behind the old ice cream shop. I drove by the other day when I was trying to show Ivy all the fun places we used to hang out. It looks completely different now."

"We'll start there, and hopefully, with these, we'll figure it out. I've looked the spell over a dozen times, as has Finn. There are no ingredients. If we're in the exact spot where we lost our memories and I say the spell, our memories should return."

It was nerve-racking. Finn had explained that his sachets would open their intuition, but only if they wanted it open. Paris knew that every single one of them had some hesitation about what they were going to do. It was very possible that it wasn't going to work.

If that were the case, then they would have to rely on Helena's journals. Only Paris didn't have much faith in them. If Helena knew what had happened, she should have written a letter explaining things. Not make them read through decades of journals. It would take forever.

It was time.

They took Ginger's car and parked it in the ice cream lot, which was empty because most of the shops hadn't opened yet for the day. Paris kept the heavy spell book in a messenger bag. Sage carried some bottles of water and snacks. Ginger was armed with a first-aid kit and an actual map in case something went wrong with their phones.

Together, they stood and stared at the forest. "We used to do this all the time as kids," Ginger said nervously. "No big deal."

"No big deal, except that we were possibly kidnapped and held for a few days," Sage pointed out. "Although, this time, we're armed."

Paris frowned. "We are?"

"Sure. We have a witch. And I have this." Sage pulled out a taser. With a laugh, Ginger reached into her pocket and pulled out a canister of mace.

"Huh. It seems that we all had very different reactions to our childhood trauma. I am not carrying a weapon of any kind."

"You got a dog," Ginger said helpfully.

Paris tried to imagine Sugar tromping through the forest with them and laughed. "All right. Here we go."

She half expected there to be another earthquake when they stepped into the forest together, but not even the birds sang to greet them.

Everything was so much more overgrown. When they were kids, the underbrush was cleared out every year so the woods would seem more inviting to tourists. It was strange to think about it now. If you wanted tourists in the woods, you put in paths and trails. Not lure them in where they might get lost.

Paris took the lead. Finn had taught her a few spells to ask the brush to move aside for them, partly so they wouldn't disturb too much of the environment but also so they could try and follow their footsteps as closely as possible. There was a stream nearby that always had boulders large enough for them to lounge on, and instinctively, that was where they headed first.

"I haven't been here since the two of you left,' Sage whispered as if she was worried that someone nearby was lurking. Nobody pointed it out. Paris didn't know about Ginger, but she was worried about the same. "It hadn't even occurred to me to come out here. Maybe it was fear, or maybe..."

"Maybe it was something keeping you out," Paris said grimly. She stopped and looked around. "This is it, except it looks like the creek bed might have run dry."

"Fireflies," Ginger said suddenly. "We came here, but we followed the fireflies."

The memory rose up, but it was hazy like she couldn't quite clean it up enough. "There was no moon," she said. "I can almost remember."

"I brought wine!" Sage gasped. "I snuck a bottle to celebrate the bonding, but I dropped it when we tried to climb over those rocks. I remember being angry that I'd wasted it."

At one point, there must have been a dam because the rocks were piled up along the wall, but time had decimated it even more. "Looks like we can go around, which is good because I most certainly do not think I can go over them anymore."

They laughed nervously and cautiously made their way across the rock rubble and deeper into the forest. After twenty years, none of the trees should have looked familiar, but Paris stopped suddenly and frowned.

It shouldn't be possible except... "That tree looks exactly the same. It has the gnarled face of an old woman. Remember? We saw it that night. I thought it was perfect for casting the spell. Like someone was watching over us."

"But we didn't stay." Ginger's voice had a faraway quality as she stroked the spell bag. "We wanted to follow the flowers."

"Flowers?" Sage frowned. "Like, blooms? I don't see any...oh."

As they turned their heads, white flowers opened, one right after the other, like dominos, until it resembled a river curving in the forest. Stunned, they were silent long after the petals had spread.

"I think we are exactly where we're supposed to be, and I'm still a little unnerved by that." She swallowed and reached out to grab their hands. "Should we follow the flowers?"

"See it through." Ginger shook just a little. "We need to see it through."

Slowly, they waded through the waist-night flowers. They moved with the spell that Paris had cast, so not a single delicate petal was broken. It felt like hours passed until the ground pulsed beneath them. Instantly, they stopped.

"That's it." Sage sounded like she was going to cry as she looked in front of them. They'd made it. "We went in that cave. My idea. Ginger, you called me an idiot and said a bear was probably using it. Paris, you said there hadn't ever been a bear sighting and decided it was probably a mountain lion. We went in anyway, but...I can't remember. I can't remember what was inside."

Paris couldn't either, and Ginger didn't offer anything else. Instead, they slowly made the climb over the loose rubble toward the mouth of the cave. When she turned around, she gasped.

The flowers were closing up. Either the forest didn't want the women to find their way out, or they didn't want anyone to follow them.

When they entered the cave, darkness closed around them. The early morning chill no longer touched them. Instead, there was a strange warmth radiating from the cave walls.

"This ringing any bells?" Ginger said nervously. "Did we just sit in the dark and let Paris perform the spell? I feel like that was something we might have done."

"Hold on. I can do this," Sage muttered. There was a snap in the darkness, and a single light floated between them.

"Is that a flashlight?" Ginger asked. "Oh. That is not a flashlight."

The light hovered between them, and Sage cleared her throat. "I have some abilities. My father didn't teach me much before he died, but this happened one night when there was a blackout at the bar, and I was trying to find the electrical panel. I can apparently summon some kind of light. I know nothing about it. Knowing the fae, I'm probably stealing bits of someone's soul to do it."

"Let's not think about that," Paris said awkwardly as she pulled out the book. Kneeling on the floor of the cave, she sat the book down. "I think we're supposed to link physically. Hold hands."

Sage and Ginger bent down, and she took a deep breath. "Last chance to back out of this."

"Are you kidding? If you don't say the spell soon, the anticipation might actually give me a heart attack," Ginger snapped. "Hurry."

Sage nodded in agreement. Although Paris had lugged the book all the way, she'd only done it out of anxiety. The truth was that she'd read the incantation so many times last night that she'd memorized it.

"Beneath my feet, I call to thee. Magic that I cannot see. Return the pieces taken from us, make whole the memories scattered to dust. We embrace the bond that was turned away and make us whole in every way. I command it!"

The cave rumbled, and Sage's light exploded. Magic washed over her, and Paris, along with the other two, floated upward. Tilting her head back, she screamed.

CHAPTER 28
PARIS

"What did you do?" Sage demanded when they landed back on their feet. "That didn't bond us together. What did that do?"

"Guys?" Ginger said in a small voice. "That was not there before."

Paris's heart trembled when she looked over. Never in her life had she felt anything like that. The spell was just supposed to be some ridiculous little fun thing. They'd say the incantation, drink Sage's wine, and eat the gummy candies Ginger had brought.

But that? That had felt real.

A strange blue light imitated from the back of the cave. They slowly walked toward it and saw that it dropped nearly ten feet down into a hidden cove that hadn't been there before.

The waters didn't seem real. Everything was so blue and glittery. The surface bubbled playfully and swirled.

"No way anyone has seen this before. It would be in every pamphlet," Sage muttered. "Come on. I think we can climb down from here."

"Wait a minute, can we talk about what just happened? We

were floating in the air. That was magic. Real magic. Something happened to us. I feel..." Ginger shook her head. "I don't know how I feel, but it's different."

Paris knew what she meant. Something pulsed inside them. It was a living, breathing thing, but it felt like it was meant to be there all along.

"Helena must be a real witch. I can't believe she didn't tell me. She didn't teach me." Paris was a little annoyed. She could wield magic, and Helena had kept it secret. Could everyone wield magic? Was she not all that special?

Slowly, they climbed down the embankment. The cove was much larger than it had first appeared. Above, the cave opened, and the stars glittered from above. "Think it's safe to swim in?" Sage grinned mischievously. "I feel like skinny dipping."

"It's moving quickly. Cave rivers are notorious for strong undercurrents. We have no idea where the water is going or how deep it is. I wouldn't risk it," Ginger said uncertainty. "We could get sucked down into a tunnel."

They wandered along the edge, and the more they walked, the faster the water seemed to move. There was another opening at the other side of the cave, creating a tunnel, and they exited out only to stop short. The water ended in a large waterfall that fell at least twenty feet below.

On her hands and knees, Sage carefully crawled as far as she could go and looked over. "There are people below."

"People? Like tourists? My mother will kill me if she finds out I snuck out again at night. I'm already grounded, remember?"

"I can't tell. They're dancing around a circle like...um, Paris? I think they're doing some kind of spell."

"What? I want to see." There wasn't enough room for her to climb to the edge with Sage. "How many witches do you think are in Silver Mist Cove?"

"Cove. Do you think the town is named after this place? I've never heard anyone talk about it."

"I have a bad feeling. Something doesn't feel right. Oh. Crap." Quickly, Sage scrambled back. *"They saw me."*

"They can't get to us. We're way up here," Paris pointed out, but she also noticed a strange feeling inside her. Like something was tugging at her. *"We should go anyway. Helena will be Furious if she finds out I took a real book of magic."*

Uneasy, they made their way back into the cove and up the embankment. When they reached the mouth, Paris saw that the strange flowers had closed up. There was no path to follow, but they quietly made their way away from the cave.

And then they heard the first rustle of movement behind them.

Fear welled up inside her, without even understanding why or how she knew that they were in danger.

They were being hunted.

"THERE YOU LADIES ARE! We have been looking everywhere for you! The sheriff is not too happy with you, Ms. Hollyman. No, sirree."

Calmly, Paris opened her eyes and looked over at the mouth of the cave. Deputy Dash stood there, his flashlight cutting through the darkness. Sage's light had gone out, and they stood next to her.

How long they'd been like that, she had no idea, but at least her feet were firmly on the floor, and she was no longer screaming.

"Deputy," Ginger smiled. She was oddly calm. They all were. So many of the missing pieces had fit back together. "Are we trespassing? This felt like public property."

"No. Finn called, frantic. Said he couldn't find you.

Sheriff wanted me to keep it a secret. He didn't want a repeat of what happened all those years ago. I'm just glad it didn't take three days to find you. What are you even doing here?"

His lies came out smoothly, but when Paris looked at his face, she no longer saw the charming, bumbling deputy. She saw the face of the man who'd held her down and covered her nose with a rag. She heard the voice of the monsters that haunted her.

She saw Darren's partner.

"Just exploring some of the places we used to go," Sage sighed and reached up to touch the stone. "It's so pretty here. I can't believe we don't do tours here. Maybe we should start. We could make a killing."

"Now, I don't think that's a good idea. Silver Mist needs to keep some secrets." Dash jerked his head. "Time to go, ladies."

"Why? Are we breaking any laws?"

"Like I said, Finn called..." his voice trailed off with Paris moved to the side. Behind them, the cove had opened once again, filling the back with a lovely blue light.

The moment Dash realized it was all over, the smile dropped from his face, and it twisted with ugliness. "So, you found your way back here after all," he snarled.

"We did." Bending down, Paris picked up the book and closed it.

Dash narrowed his eyes. "She managed to get her book back after all. We held it for years, you know. Helena was not as powerful as she liked to think."

"She was more powerful than you. And so are we. We know what you did, Dash. Capturing us. Drugging us. Experimenting on us to try and sever our bond with the ley line. At the time, I didn't understand. I had no idea what we'd bonded with. None of us did. You didn't have to terrify us like that. Torture us."

"Maybe I liked it," Dash grinned.

Oh, he'd definitely liked it. Paris remembered it well. When Darren had suggested that he and Dash should let them go, Dash had laughed maniacally. He didn't want to sever the bond from the afar. He wanted to do it up close and personal.

He wanted to hear their screams.

"Death would have done it," Dash grunted. "Everyone knew it. Kill you and Helena, and the ley line was ours for the taking."

The ley line. The magic ran beneath their feet. Helena had been the guardian, and when Paris had tried to bond with her friends, she'd somehow taken the bond from Helena. Bonded herself, Ginger, and Sage with the ley line.

Named themselves the new guardians.

"I guess it's not too late to rectify that mistake." Dash pulled out his gun. "Bullets kill witches, too, you know."

He pulled the trigger, and the cave went silent. The sound of the shot never even reached their ears. Magic blasted from Paris, and the air turned so thick around them that, for a moment, she couldn't breathe.

"Not now," Paris whispered. Around her, she could see the colored tendrils of magic rising up from the darkness. The ley line. She had no idea what she'd done with the bond, but guardianship of the ley line had always been hers. Helena knew it. When she looked into the mirror all those years ago, this was what she'd been seeing. The magic that belonged to everyone. The magic that she was supposed to protect.

They were supposed to protect. "Not ever. This place is ours, and you can't have it."

Sage flicked her fingers, and the bullet turned and flew backward.

Right into Dash's shoulder.

He bellowed with pain, but he didn't go down. Instead, flames shot out from his palms.

"You," Sage snarled. "You set fire to my bar! How dare you!"

"Nobody survives my fire." Sweat appeared on his forehead. Paris didn't know if it was pain or the energy from using magic. "Better this way. No need to explain a pile of ash in the middle of nowhere."

"I don't think so," Ginger said calmly, moving to his side.

"You're human," he laughed. "What are you going to do?"

"This." She aimed her canister and sprayed him directly in the eyes with her mace. Dash screamed, and his fire extinguished as he clawed at his eyes.

While he spewed obscenities, Paris tripped him and pulled out her phone. "Look at that. A full set of bars. I guess we should call the sheriff and end this."

Sage stood over him, her taser in hand. "Move," she hissed. "I dare you."

It was over. They knew the truth.

And Paris really had no idea where they were going to go from there.

CHAPTER 29

PARIS

The next twelve hours went by quickly. Finn reached them before Sheriff Dobbs. After checking them over to make certain they were all right, he did something to Dash that helped both slow the bleeding and keep him quiet.

And, Paris suspected, something else that made Dash sing like a canary when the sheriff did arrive. Not about what happened twenty-five years ago, but just admitting that Paris, Sage, and Ginger needed to die, and he was more than happy to do it.

After that, they didn't have to explain much. The sheriff took one look at them and immediately knew they were the new guardians of the ley line. It was strange being shown such reverent respect. He tipped his hat and muttered that he would take care of everything.

It wasn't an apology, but it was something.

Finn drove Paris back to the manor, but she couldn't stop asking questions. "So the ley line just shut down after we took over the guardianship? Or did we not take over guardianship until Helena died? What does that even mean? Do we control the magic? I cannot control that much magic. Just asking it to give us back our memories nearly knocked me out!"

"Paris," Finn interrupted quietly. "What happened? Why did Dash and Darren kidnap you?"

Blinking, she realized that she hadn't even told him what happened. They walked into the kitchen, and he started making tea.

"After I did the bonding spell, the cove just opened up. It felt like it was welcoming us, and we peered over the edge of the waterfall. Sage saw people below it. Dash and Darren." She paused. "Hold on, she said there was a circle of people. That means there had to have been more. They spotted her, and we ran. Mostly, we didn't want to get in trouble, but when they tracked us in the forest, I knew it was trouble. They were dangerous."

"What did they do?"

"They were trying to sever the bond between us and the ley line. It gave us horrific hallucinations. I guess after a few days, Darren decided to let us go. I remember that Dash had gone out to get more food. Darren led us back to the edge of the forest and took our memories."

"He must have lived with that guilt all this time," Finn mused. "And when he knew you would return, he wanted to come clean. Dash must have killed him."

Paris stared at him. "Finn, we never even asked. Of course, Dash killed Darren. We need to get to the sheriff's station right now and tell him. Ask Dash ourselves. Is there a spell to help reveal the truth?"

"There are, but I've never found one that's reliable. Sometimes, we don't know the truth."

His voice softened, and she reached for him. "Like whether you love someone?"

"Knowing that we weren't supposed to be together has a way of altering any other emotions." He cleared his throat. "You're bonded with the town itself, Paris. Does that change how you feel about me? About what you want in the future?"

"If I had to, I would give up all the magic in the world for you, Finn."

"I feel the same, but it's not going to come to that. It'll take a while to transition here full-time, but I can do it. What about you? Your interior design business? I don't know that there's going to be a big market for that here."

"It's not just about the design, Finn. It's about making the space a sanctuary. There is definitely a market for that in a place like this. Silver Mist Cove is meant to be a sanctuary. I can help it become that again." A thought occurred to her. "The name of the town must come from that cove. Have you ever seen it?"

"No. Maybe it's something only the ley line guardians can see." The tea kettled whistled. "Tea, and then we'll go to the sheriff's station, and then you're going to rest. I don't think you've slept in two nights."

It was true, and she was starting to feel the frayed edges of exhaustion. "Rest will be good. There is still so much to do."

By the time Paris and Finn reached the station, Dash was in a jail cell. Everyone was muttering quietly or staring off into space like they didn't know what to do with themselves. Dash had been one of them. It was hard for them to grasp the darkness inside of him.

"Paris, you shouldn't be here," Sheriff Dobbs said heavily. "The next few weeks are not going to be easy on you. The whole town is going to want to talk to you."

"That isn't my current worry. I need to know. Did Dash kill Darren?"

Dobbs nodded. "He did. He told us that Darren had confessed that he was going to tell. Dash killed him in the house. He tried to drag Darren's body out, but something had spooked him. He thought he saw a woman there."

Marigold. Paris kept that to herself. They'd made a deal, after all.

"And what happened twenty-five years ago? Did he admit to kidnapping us?"

The sheriff muttered something under his breath before he finally nodded. "He did. He said that he and Darren heard you cast the spell to bond with the ley line and decided to see if they could take it from you. Darren let you go and wiped your memories. This town has a lot to apologize to you for. I guess I do as well."

"And the others? Did he say who he was working with?"

"Others? No," Sheriff Dobbs frowned. "It was just him and Darren. Why? Did you remember someone else?"

"No. Well, maybe. We think there might have been others nearby, but maybe they didn't have anything to do with it. No, I'm sorry. I need to go with my intuition on this. There's more to it. I just know it. Can we talk to him?"

"Paris..."

"You all thought we were lying. You practically ran us out of town. I deserve a chance to question the man who kidnapped us!"

After a moment, he sighed and nodded. "All right. Follow me."

He led them down a hallway to their holding jail cells. Dash was the only one back there. He just sat on one side and stared at the other.

Paris wanted to get closer, but Finn anchored an arm

around her waist. "Ask your questions from here," he whispered in her ear. "I don't want you close enough where he can touch you."

"Dash, I need to ask you some questions about the night you kidnapped Sage, Ginger, and me. We deserve answers."

"Answers," Dash said and looked at her. His eyes had trouble focusing on her. "I will give you answers."

"Were you working alone?"

"I was working with Darren."

His voice was flat and devoid of emotion. Her stomach fluttered with unease. "You said you were talking to them. Who is them?"

"Darren."

"And?"

"Just Darren."

"You told them that you could just kill us." Finn's grip tightened on her waist, but Paris pushed on. "Who did you tell?"

"Darren."

"Did you kill Darren?"

"I killed Darren."

Frustrated, Paris looked up at Finn. "Something is wrong with him. He sounds like he's under a spell."

"I agree, but I don't see or feel anything attached to them. Has he been alone this whole time?"

"Yup. I was the one who brought him back here. I haven't allowed any of the deputies to see him," Dobbs said as he stroked his chin. "He does sound different. You think he's lying?"

"I don't know. I guess not. I only remember the two of them."

"There you go." Dobbs snapped his fingers. "He probably did something to himself to help him get a lighter sentence. Maybe an insanity plea. Still a human court. He starts blabbering about magic and ley lines; they'll definitely plead insanity."

That hadn't occurred to Paris, but it made sense. Still, she couldn't shake the nagging feeling that there was something that she was missing. "All right. Now I'm tired. Let's go home."

Dobbs looked at them. "You two gonna stick around?"

Finn rested his head against hers, and she smiled. "Yeah. We're going to stick around."

A WEEK LATER, there was a full moon. Paris, Ginger, and Sage returned to the cove. This time, they didn't need to rely on anything to help them remember the way. The forest opened up on its own, blooming in a path to the cove.

They didn't bring any spell books. Just a bottle of wine and some gummies, and they had the kind of night they'd wanted to have twenty-five years ago.

Beneath them, the ley line pulsed like it was happy to see them.

Afterward, they decided that while they didn't really understand their duties as guardians of the ley line, they weren't going to run. They would figure out what it meant, one day at a time.

Afterward, Paris pulled out Annabelle's spell jar. With Finn's help, she'd put it back together. Annabelle had wanted peace, and Paris wanted to give it to her. Darren had haunted their nightmares, but in the end, he'd wanted to do the right thing. Paris wasn't sure she could forgive him, but Annabelle had done nothing wrong but fallen in love with a man; she would help the woman get peace.

Finn was still going through the journals. Paris hadn't touched them yet. She just wasn't ready. In her mind, Helena had done more harm than good.

You try raising two hormonal teenagers with magical destinies and see how you do.

Paris blinked at the witch's voice and frowned. That was no memory. "Oh no," she said softly. "Don't you dare start talking to me now, from the grave. I will never forgive you."

Then it's a good thing I care more about you than your forgiveness, isn't it?

Oh, great.

EPILOGUE

Ginger wrapped her arms around herself while she rocked back and forth. Her mother's rocking chair had seen a lot of use, and growing up, Ginger had always teased her about it. There she was, the most popular psychic in a town full of psychics and, rocking on her rocking chair like an old woman.

It turned out there was something soothing about the back-and-forth motion, and Ginger needed soothing. She was human. No real psychic abilities. No magic. No fey heritage, And tethered to a magical pipeline in town with a werewolf teenage daughter,

Who was heaven knows where?

How had her life come to this?

She'd been determined to have a normal life. She went to college. Tried to put her past behind her. Fell in love and married.

Then was abandoned three months after they were married. She discovered she was pregnant at four months. He couldn't even be bothered to sign divorce papers. She had to prove that she'd been abandoned to the courts. Talk about humiliation.

Then, her daughter turned thirteen, and her eyes shifted from their normal dark brown hues to yellow.

At first, Ginger had been sure that it was a trick of the light. Then, her daughter started freaking out. Felt like there was something inside of her.

They saw doctors. Psychiatrists. The psychiatrists used all kinds of professional terminology, but Ginger knew they were wrong. It wasn't in her head. There was something happening to her child.

Finally, in a last-minute desperate attempt, she hired a private investigator to find her ex-husband's family. It took six months and the rest of her savings.

She'd found the former mother-in-law that she'd never met, who looked at her frostily from her mansion-style home and told Ginger she must have been mistaken. Her son didn't have a wife and child.

When she walked back to her car, devoid of hope, an older man had fallen into step next to her. He hadn't said a word, but he opened the car door for her and told her to have a nice trip back.

And when she got in, he slipped her a piece of paper and walked away.

It had one word on it.

Werewolf.

It didn't seem possible, but here they were, a year later, in the only place she could think of that might have werewolves.

Back to her hometown.

A howl went up in the distance, and she shivered.

Not her daughter. Not Ivy. Despite being a werewolf, Ivy

233

hadn't shifted yet. Privately, she hoped that she never would. Ivy deserved a normal life.

The howl sounded again, this time closer.

Ginger stood and gripped the column of the porch. Her daughter had been disappearing at night. Was that her? Howling in the woods? All alone?

A crash sounded, and Ginger whipped her head around. Before she could scream, an enormous black wolf skidded to a stop in front of her. It's eyes locked onto hers.

Hunger.

"Mom!"

"Ivy! Stay back, honey." Ginger watched in fear as her daughter, panting, ran her way.

Toward the wolf.

Was she chasing?

"What are you doing? Stay back!" Stumbling down the steps, she put herself between the wolf and her daughter. "Go inside. Through the back. Now."

The wolf tossed his head back and howled. Then, with a quick shake of its head, the wolf was gone.

And a very naked man lay in the grass.

"It's a werewolf. I found a werewolf!" Ivy said triumphantly. "I've been tracking him for a few weeks now. I knew I could smell him."

That's what her daughter had been doing? And here Ginger had hoped she was partying with some of the other teenagers. "And you brought him back here. That's nice." Taking a deep breath, she walked toward the man. "Sir? Are you all right?"

With a groan, he lifted himself and stood. Ginger was about to ask her daughter to avert her eyes, but the shock had rendered her speechless.

The man shook his head and grinned. "This isn't exactly how I planned to introduce myself. I'm Zane."

Her heart skipped a beat. "The man next door."

"Right. So, can I borrow a cup of sugar?"

CONTINUE THE MAGIC: Read Book Two – The Mother's Legacy

Thank you for joining Paris on her journey through grief, awakening magic, and rediscovering love. But the story is far from over. In *The Mother's Legacy*, Ginger steps into the spotlight—facing the shadows of her past, the depths of a mother's love, and the secrets she's kept even from herself. As Silver Mist Cove trembles under the weight of change, a new danger rises—and Ginger's legacy may be the only thing standing in its way.

If you're ready for more coven bonds, elemental magic, and the return of characters you've come to love (plus a few new ones who will steal your heart), turn the page and begin the next chapter.

The Mother's Legacy is waiting for you.

THANK YOU

I hope you enjoyed reading this as much as I enjoyed creating it. If you did and would like to help me get this out into the world, reviews are the most significant way you can help. As an indie author, it is hard to be found among the masses of books released every day, and I appreciate your reviews so much.

The most impactful is Amazon. Goodreads and Bookbub are great second choices.

If you would like to join my newsletter to stay in touch, you can do so here. I send out lots of freebies to my list.

Thank you to my sisters and my ARC readers for your feedback. I so appreciate you all. Thank you to my husband, my daughters, and my parents for their support.

xoxo

Lyssa

About the Author

Lyssa Lund is a writer, wife, mother of four grown daughters, and proud grandmother to three granddaughters and one grandson. She lives in Minnesota with her husband, Craig, and a beautiful Borzoi, Isa, where long winters give her the perfect excuse to dive deep into writing stories.

When she's not writing, Alyssa loves cooking and baking for her family, crafting, golfing, reading, and singing in a blues band.

Her books invite readers into atmospheric towns where every woman holds a story worth telling.

She adores reader feedback at hello@lyssaLund.com

www.lyssalund.com

Also By Lyssa Lund

Shadows Of Dark And Light

A Touch Of Prophesy

The Dark King's Heart

The Sylvan Wilds

Witches Will Rise - coming soon

The Borderland Guardians

The Blizzard Crossing

Beyond Aorel

The Hall Of Divinity

Realms Of Destiny Series

The Lost Heir Of Isla

Kingpin Of Topree

Maya Rodgers Mysteries

Deadly Dynasty

Ink and Blood

Brushed By Danger

Sleight Of Death

Lake Minnetonka Cozy Mysteries

Secrets Buried

Petals Of Peril

Party Sparks

FREEBIE

As a Thank you for reading my book, I'd love to offer you another title for free.

A Touch Of Prophesy

You are invited to download this book as my gift here. Or you can get it @ www.lyssalund.com